1967

1964

Classic Tales

from

MODERN SPAIN

Selection, translation and edition by

WILLIAM E. COLFORD

1314

BARRON'S EDUCATIONAL SERIES, INC.

GREAT NECK, NEW YORK

For my son, Robert

INTRODUCTION

THE WORD "CLASSIC" as applied to this collection of short stories has the same connotation as in the companion volume in this series, CLASSIC TALES FROM SPANISH AMERICA. They are stories that are known and loved by every literate person as part of the cultural heritage of the nation, in the way that many of the stories of our American authors have become "classics": Washington Irving's *Rip Van Winkle* and *The Legend of Sleepy Hollow*; the tales of Edgar Allan Poe; Edward Everett Hale's *The Man Without a Country*; Joel Chandler Harris' stories about *Uncle Remus* in the South; and the poignant vignettes of big-city life sketched by O. Henry, such as *The Gift of the Magi* and *The Last Leaf*. It is Spanish stories of the same calibre that are presented—most of them for the first time in English—in this collection.

While the development of the short story on our side of the Atlantic coincides with the growth of the American republics and is a reflection of our new cultures, in Spain its origins are very old indeed. It was the ancient culture of the Arabs, brought by the Moors who crossed over to Spain from North Africa in the eighth century and remained for more than seven hundred years, that gave rise to the early and persistent popularity of the short story in the Iberian peninsula. The vast storehouse of Oriental tales brought from India, Persia and Arabia was opened by Alfonso the Wise, thirteenth-century Castilian monarch, who ordered that one of these collections, the *Book* of *Kalila and Digma*, be translated from Arabic into Spanish in 1251, the first such anthology in any modern European language. Many others followed, and through Spain the literary treasures of the Orient passed to the rest of Europe.

But it was the nephew of Alfonso the Wise, Don Juan Manuel, who was the first to compose such tales himself. His book, written in 1335, is called *Count Lucanor*, for such is the name of the young nobleman who asks advice of his steward Patronio and is answered by a moral tale or "example." The whole work has a distinctly Oriental tone. Some of its fifty apologues, anecdotes and tales come from Spanish folklore, and others are based (in part) on earlier sources such as the *Arabian Nights* and Aesop's *Fables*. One of the most noteworthy tales is "What Happened to a Young Man Who Married a Very Unruly and Ill-Tempered Wife," which is, of course, the prototype of Shakespeare's *The Taming of the Shrew*. Whether the English bard came upon this story in translation is not known.

Still another literary "first" for Spain in the development of the short story was the picaresque novel, which is essentially a series of short stories woven around the central figure—a poor lad who serves many masters and later recounts these adventures. The anonymous *Lazarillo de Tormes* (1554) was the grandfather of all picaresque tales in Spain and elsewhere in Europe.

In 1613 Cervantes again used the Oriental, moral-giving term "exemplary" in the title of the twelve short stories he called the *Exemplary Novels*. (He employed the word "novel" for a written, fictional narrative, and "story" for a commonly-told oral tale.) These twelve literary gems deal with many subjects—psychological, picaresque, satirical—and are entirely unrelated to one another. The work, in modern terminology, is a collection of short stories. They are truly original, "neither imitated nor stolen," Cervantes tells us in his preface to them. "My imagination sired them, and my pen gave them birth." Their success throughout Europe is attested to by their prompt translation into the major continental languages.

Later in the seventeenth century, short stories followed the prevalent obscure, baroque style. The fantastic *Dreams* of Quevedo are an outstanding example. And in the eighteenth century another kind of moralizing story began to flourish—the "sketch." This described contemporary scenes and characters typical of the times. Although this "periodical" type of article came to Spain from England (Addison and Steele) and from France (Mercier and Jouy), it was essentially a return of the earlier Spanish picaresque influence—now changed in tone—to the land of its origin.

We come now to the period covered by this present collection of translations—the nineteenth and twentieth centuries. As illiteracy in Spain diminished, a greater reading public bought newspapers and magazines. Short, descriptive articles were particularly adapted to this type of reading public, and the *cuadro de costumbres* emerged. The word *cuadro* means "picture," and at first these articles were merely descriptive of the customs of a locality. Gradually, however, characters were added to give more appeal and substance to the articles, which ultimately became short stories. Initially, a critical tone prevailed in most of them, and the authors of such stories often used them as vehicles for suggested reforms of customs and manners. Works by the two most renowned of these *costumbristas*, Larra and Mesonero Romanos, are included in this collection.

The Romantic movement, with its profound interest in folklore, legends, historical details and sentimental antiquarianism, is represented in stories by Bécquer and Fernán Caballero. The latter also became the first outstanding novelist in modern Spain. Many of the best Spanish novelists wrote short stories also (as did Melville and Hawthorne, for example, in our country) and thus are represented in this collection; but some (like our James Fenimore Cooper, for instance) are noted almost exclusively for their novels, and therefore have not been included.

As the nineteenth century advanced, realism—and, to some extent, naturalism—came to the fore in Spain. Regionalism, too, was strong in the Iberian peninsula, for it is criss-crossed by many mountain chains that divide it into self-contained units. Indeed, Spain is—after Switzerland—the most mountainous country in Europe. Small wonder, then, that regionalism—even to the point of separatism—is so strong in Spain.

It is the aim of this collection to present to English-speaking readers representative stories by outstanding modern authors chosen from the many regions of Spain. Galicia, in the northwest, with the feminine contours of its gently rolling hills and its misty, Celtic landscape, is represented by Valle-Inclán and Pardo Bazán. In the north, the austere Asturian coast along the Bay of Biscay has as its representatives Clarín, Pérez de Ayala and Palacio Valdés, while the rugged Basque country appears in a story by Pío Baroja. Unamuno, also a Basque, transcends all boundaries: his contribution to the collection is an ironic, philosophical fantasy.

The Mediterranean coast—called in Spain "The Levant"—has as its contributors Azorín and Blasco Ibáñez, while the Balearic Islands are represented by the contemporary author Alfredo Marqueríe. In the south, Andalusia, with its gypsies, bandits and sun-drenched plains, appears in stories by Alarcón and Fernán Caballero. As for central Spain, modern Madrid is seen in a story by the humorous Gómez de la Serna, old Madrid is portrayed by Larra and Mesonero Romanos, and Bécquer (though a Sevillian) contributes a fantastic tale of old Toledo. The presentation of the stories, then, is geographic rather than chronological, for this seemed the best way to introduce the English-speaking reader to the many facets of the spirit of Spain.

Rather than go into further detail about each author at this time, it has seemed best to interpolate the biographical sketches of the authors and their place in Spanish letters immediately before each selection; in this way they will serve to place the writer and his work into proper focus just before the reader starts the story. It is to be hoped that students of Comparative Literature, as well as the general reader, will be drawn to further exploration of the wealth of short stories by modern Spanish authors, who rank with the world's finest writers in this genre.

W. E. C.

New York, 1964.

CONTENTS

xi

Ramón del Valle-Inclán (1866–1936)

. . . is the great stylist of the Generation of 1898—the group of writers who came into prominence during the period of agonizing introspection and self-criticism that followed the loss of Spain's last colonial possessions as a result of the Spanish-American War. Unlike many others, who concentrated on problems of the present and future, Valle-Inclán looked toward the past, particularly the nostalgic past of his native Galicia. This northwestern corner of Spain retains much of the spirit of the Celts who came to the region in pre-Christian times: their folklore, bagpipes, superstitions and mysticism are reminiscent of Ireland. Even the soft, lyrical, Galician speech (akin to Portuguese) differs considerably from standard Castilian. There is quite a large body of literature in the language of this region; Valle-Inclán, however, writes for the larger Spanish-speaking world on both sides of the Atlantic, and uses Castilian with an admixture of Galician vocabulary and syntax. This produces a magical, musical, poetic prose that defies description—a style, moreover, that blends beautifully with the brooding, tragic atmosphere of his stories.

Don Ramón himself was thin and ascetic-looking. He had a long, scraggly beard and always wore a cape to conceal the loss of his left arm. When someone dared to bring up the subject of this missing member, he would tell a different story each time: a jealous husband shot him, and the arm had to be amputated; a tiger clawed him in the jungle; or a dozen other fantastic tales.

Valle-Inclán was also a poet, dramatist and novelist, but it is in the field of the novelette and the short story that he excels. His four *Sonatas* (1902–1905), one for each season of the year, purport to be the memoirs of the love affairs of a Galician nobleman, the Marqués de Bradomín, "ugly, Catholic, and sentimental," in the author's words. He was a haughty, cynical, sensual and refined but decadent aesthete who consented to allow himself to be loved. In a trilogy of novels in dialogue, which he called *Barbaric Comedies* (1907, 1908, 1922), the background is again Galician and the protagonist is a relative of the Marqués: Don Manuel Montenegro, a nineteenth-century feudal baron, despotic and erotic, who lived in a crumbling old manor house.

It is in Valle-Inclán's collection of short stories entitled *Shady Garden* (1903) that his most typical tales are to be found. "My Sister Antonia," which is set in old Santiago de Compostela, a shrine for pilgrimages since the Middle Ages, contains all the elements that have placed Valle-Inclán in the forefront of modern Spanish letters as a stylist and a storyteller: its evocation of the aristocratic, mediaeval past, its atmosphere of mystery and dimly-recalled sensations, and above all its exquisite, musical language in which each word is carefully chosen for its sound and rhythm in the sentence. The introduction to the collection sets the mood for this moving tale:

MY GRANDMOTHER had an old servant whose name was Micaela la Galana. She died when I was still a child. I remember that she used to spend hours spinning at an open window, and that she knew many stories about saints, souls in torment, goblins, and robbers. I shall tell you now those she used to tell to me as her wrinkled fingers turned the spindle. Those stories, filled with glowing, tragic mystery, frightened me at night during my childhood years: hence I have not forgotten them. From time to time they still rise up to haunt my memory, and as if a cold, silent wind were blowing over them, they have the long-drawn rustle of dried-out leaves. The rustle of an old, abandoned garden. A shady garden.

My Sister Antonia

SANTIAGO DE GALICIA was once one of the world's shrines, and people there still keep their eyes ever alert for miracles. . . .

2

One afternoon my sister Antonia took me by the hand to go to the cathedral. Antonia was much older than I. She was tall and pale, with dark eyes and a rather sad smile. She died while I was still a child, but how I remember her voice and her smile, and her ice-cold hand as she took me to the cathedral each afternoon! Above all, I remember her eyes and their bright, tragic glow as they watched a certain student who used to stroll in the cathedral courtyard muffled up in his blue cape. I was afraid of that student: he was tall and gaunt, with a corpse-like face and tiger eyes—terrible eyes beneath thin, scowling eyebrows. His knee-bones creaked as he walked, and made him seem even more like the dead. My mother hated him, and to avoid seeing him she used to keep the windows of our house shuttered on the side that faced the Platerías courtyard. That afternoon, I recall, he was strolling back and forth as he did every afternoon, muffled up in his blue cape. He overtook us at the cathedral door, and putting his skeleton hand out from beneath his cape he took some holy water and offered it to my sister, who was trembling. Antonia looked at him imploringly as he murmured through a smile:

"I am desperate!"

3

We went into a chapel where some old women were praying at the Stations of the Cross. It is a huge, gloomy chapel, filled with sounds that rise from the floor and echo from the Romanesque vault. When I was a child that chapel gave me a feeling of rustic peace. It used to afford me a very personal kind of pleasure, like the foliage of an old chestnut tree, like vines growing outside doorways, like a hermit's haunt in the hills. In the afternoon there was always a group of old women praying at the Stations of the Cross. Their voices, blending in a murmur of religious fervor, swelled beneath the arches and seemed to brighten the rose windows like the setting sun. There rose the sound of a flight of high-pitched, pious prayers, the soft shuffling of feet across the floor, and the tinkling of a little silver bell shaken by the young acolyte as he held a lighted candle over the shoulder of the chaplain, who slowly read from his breviary the Passion of Our Lord. Oh, Chapel of Corticela, when will this soul of mine—so old, so tired—immerse itself again in thy soothing shadows!

4

Night had fallen, and it was drizzling as we crossed the cathedral courtyard on our way home. Our vestibule was wide and dark; my sister must have been afraid, for she ran all the way up the stairs without letting go of my hand. As we went inside we saw our mother crossing the hallway and disappearing through an open door. Without knowing why, I was afraid and bewildered. I raised my eyes and looked up at my sister; without a word she bent down and kissed me. Despite my complete ignorance of life I had guessed Antonia's secret, and I felt its weight upon me like a mortal sin as I crossed that hallway. Smoke was rising from an oil lamp with a broken chimney: the flame was shaped like two horns, and it reminded me of the Devil. That night as I lay in bed in the darkness the resemblance kept growing on me, and would not let me sleep. It came back to trouble me many other nights.

5

Several rainy afternoons followed. The student strolled in the courtyard during lulls in the rain, but my sister did not go out to pray at vespers. Sometimes as I sat studying my lessons in the parlor, which was full of the aroma of withered roses, I would open the window slightly to see him. He would be walking all alone, smiling nervously, and in the dusk he looked so much like a dead man that it frightened me. Trembling, I would come away from the window; but I kept on visualizing him and could not learn my lesson. In the big parlor, closed off and hollow-sounding, I could hear the creaking of his knees and leg bones as he walked. . . . The cat yowled outside the door, and it seemed to me that its caterwauling formed the student's name:

Máximo Bretal!

6

Bretal is a hamlet in the hills, not far from Santiago. The old men there still wear pointed caps and homespun coats, the old women spin in the stables because these are warmer than the houses, and the sacristan holds school in the courtyard of the church. Beneath his rod children still learn the legal-style handwriting used by mayors and town clerks, and read in chorus from real estate deeds that belonged to an old landed family long since departed. Máximo Bretal was a member of that family. He came to Santiago to study theology. At first, an old woman who sold honey used to bring him a weekly supply of corn bread and bacon. With other impoverished young men studying for the priesthood he lived in an inn where they paid just for their lodging. Máximo Bretal had already taken Minor Orders when he came to our house to be my tutor in Latin grammar. Out of charity, the curate of Bretal had recommended him to my mother. An old woman wearing a cowl came to thank her, and brought her a basket of tangy-sweet apples as a present. In one of those apples (people said later) must have been the spell that bewitched my sister.

7

Our mother was deeply devout and did not believe in omens or in witchcraft, but sometimes she pretended to believe in order to explain away the passion that was consuming her daughter. At about this time Antonia was beginning to have an air about her that was not of this world, like the student from Bretal. I remember her embroidering far back in the parlor, as indistinct as if she were reflected from deep inside a mirror. She had a deathly pallor, and her slow movements seemed to respond to the rhythm of a different life; she spoke in a hushed voice, and had a far-away smile. All white and sad, and so pale she seemed to have a halo like the moon, she was shrouded in some sombre secret. . . . And I remember my mother drawing aside the drapes in the doorway to peer at her, and then tiptoeing away!

8

The afternoons of pale gold sunshine returned, and my sister took me as before to the Chapel of Corticela to pray with the old women. I used to tremble lest the student appear again and stretch his phantom hand, dripping holy water, across our path. In my fright, I would look up at my sister: her lips were trembling. Máximo Bretal, who was in the courtyard every afternoon, would disappear as we drew near; then, as we crossed the nave of the cathedral, we would see him appear again among the shadows of the arches. We would enter the chapel, and he would kneel down on the steps at the doorway to kiss the flagstones where my sister Antonia had just walked. He would remain there kneeling like a statue on a sepulchre, his cape hanging from his shoulders and his hands clasped before him. One afternoon as we were going out I saw his spectral arm stretch out before me and clutch a corner of Antonia's skirt between his fingers:

"I am desperate! You must listen to me, you must realize how much I am suffering. . . . Don't you want to look at me any more?"

Antonia, faded as a flower, murmured:

"Leave me alone, Don Máximo!"

"I won't. You are mine . . . your soul is mine. I do not want your body: death will come to claim it soon. Look at me . . . let your eyes confess in mine! Look at me!"

And his wax-like hand pulled so hard at my sister's skirt that he ripped it. But her innocent eyes peered into the depths of his gleaming, terrible eyes. That night in the darkness I recalled the scene, and wept as if my sister had left us and run away from home. . . .

9

I continued to study my Latin lessons in the parlor filled with the aroma of withered roses. Some afternoons my mother would go through the parlor like a wraith and disappear into the drawing room. I would hear her sink with a sigh into one corner of the big crimson damask-covered sofa, and I could make out the faint clicking of her rosary beads as she prayed. My mother was very beautiful, with her white skin and blonde hair, and she always wore a silk dress. One hand was covered by a black glove because two of her fingers were missing; the other, lovely as a camelia, was adorned with rings. This was always the hand we kissed, and the one with which she caressed us. The other, the one with the black glove, she kept hidden in the folds of her lace handkerchief, and only when she crossed herself would she reveal it completely, so sad and dark against the whiteness of her forehead, against the rose color of her lips, against her Madonna-like bosom.

Buried in the drawing-room sofa, my mother prayed; and I, in order to take advantage of the daylight that came in through the half-opened balcony blinds, would study my Latin at the other end of the room, with my grammar opened upon one of those old tables that have an inlaid checkerboard top. It was very hard to see anything in that big parlor, closed off and hollow-sounding. Sometimes when my mother came back into it after her prayers she would tell me to open the balcony blinds wider; I would obey in silence, and would take advantage of the opportunity to look out into the courtyard where the student was strolling in the twilight haze. That afternoon, just as I was looking at him, he disappeared; I went back to reciting my Latin lesson, and there was a knock at the parlor door. It was a Franciscan friar who had recently returned from the Holy Land.

10

Padre Bernardo had at one time been my mother's confessor, and when he came back from his pilgrimage he did not forget to bring her a rosary made of olive pits from Mount Olivet. He was a little old man with a large, bald head, and resembled the Romanesque saints carved on the main portal of the cathedral. That afternoon was his second visit to our house since his return to his convent in Santiago. When I saw him come in I left my grammar and ran to kiss his hand. I remained on my knees, looking up at him and waiting for his blessing: it seemed to me that his fingers formed a pair of horns. I closed my eyes in fright at that trick of the Devil! With a shudder I realized that it was one of his tricks, like those found in the stories about the saints that I was beginning to read aloud to my mother and Antonia; it was a trick to make me sin, like the one in the story of the life of St. Anthony of Padua.

Padre Bernardo, whom my grandmother would have called a saint on earth, turned to greet my mother, his erstwhile lamb, and forgot to complete the sign of the cross over my close-cropped little head with its ears that stuck out as if they were about to take flight—a little boy's head upon which the cheerless chains of childhood weighed heavily: Latin by day, and fear of the dead by night. The friar spoke in low tones to my mother, who raised her gloved hand:

"Go outside, my child!"

11

Basilisa la Galinda, an old woman who had been my mother's nurse, was crouching outside the door. I saw her, and she caught me by the coat and put her wrinkled hand over my mouth:

"Don't make a sound, you little rascal!"

I stood staring at her, because I found in her a strange resemblance to the gargoyles on the cathedral. After a moment she gave me a gentle push:

"Go away, child!"

I wriggled my shoulders to break loose from her hand, with its deep, dark wrinkles; but I stayed beside her. We could hear the voice of the Franciscan:

"It is a matter of saving a soul. . . ."

Basilisa gave me another push:

"Go away; you mustn't listen to this. . . ."

And all humped over, she put her eye to the crack in the door. I crouched down beside her. This time she said only these words:

"Just don't you remember anything you hear, you little rascal!"

I started to laugh. It was true: she did look like a gargoyle; I couldn't decide whether it was a dog, or a cat, or a wolf, but she bore a strange resemblance to those stone figures that peer out over the courtyard from the cornice of the cathedral.

12

We heard the conversation in the parlor. The voice of the Franciscan went on for some time:

"This morning a young man tempted by the Devil came to our convent. He told me that he had had the misfortune to fall in love; in his desperation he wished

to have supernatural powers, and at midnight had in-
voked the help of Satan. The evil spirit appeared to
him amid a vast, cinder-strewn area filled with the
sound of a mighty, rushing wind caused by his bat's
wings beating beneath the stars."

We heard my mother sigh: "Oh, God!"

The friar continued:

"Satan said that if the young man signed a pact with
him he would guarantee happiness in love. The youth
hesitated, for he had been baptized a Christian, and
drove the Devil away with the sign of the cross. At
dawn this morning he came to me at our convent and
made his confession of all this. I told him he must give
up his diabolic practices, but he refused. All my advice
could not move him. His soul will be lost!"

My mother moaned again: "I'd rather see my
daughter dead!"

And the friar's voice, terrifying and mysterious, continued:

"If she were dead, he might triumph over Hell; but
with her alive, perhaps they may both be lost. . . . The
power of one poor woman like you is not enough to
fight infernal wisdom. . . ."

My mother sobbed: "With the grace of God. . . ."

There was a long silence: the friar must have been
praying as he thought of his reply. Basilisa la Galinda
held me close to her breast. We heard the sandals of the
friar, and the old woman loosened her grip on me a little
in order to rise and flee. But she stayed on, held motionless by that voice which said:

"God's grace is not always with us, my child. Like a
spring, it wells up and then runs dry. There are souls
that think only of their own salvation and that never
feel love for their fellow creatures: these are springs

run dry. Tell me, what grief has your heart felt when you heard that a Christian was in danger of damnation? What are you doing to thwart that evil pact with the powers of perdition? You deny him your daughter so he may get her from the hand of Satan!"

My mother screamed: "The Lord Jesus will prevail!"

And the friar replied in a vengeful voice:

"Love should be for all God's creatures alike. To love one's father, or son, or husband, is to love idols of clay. Without realizing it you are striking at the Cross with your evil hand, like the student from Bretal."

He must have had his arms outstretched, pointing at my mother. Then we heard a noise, as if he were coming out. Basilisa hurried away with me, and we saw a black cat pass beside us. No one saw Padre Bernardo leave. That afternoon Basilisa went to the convent, and came back with the news that he was on a mission many miles away. . . .

13

How the rain lashed at the windowpanes, and how gloomy the afternoon light was in all the rooms!

Antonia embroidered near the balcony window while our mother, stretched out on the sofa, watched her intently with the fixed, glazed stare of a statue. A great silence enveloped our souls: the only sound was the ticking of the clock. On one occasion Antonia sat dreaming, her needle poised in midair; our mother sighed, and my sister fluttered her eyelids as if she were just awakening. All the churchbells started to ring. Basilisa came in with lights; she looked behind all the doors, and barred the windows. Antonia nodded again over her embroidery; my mother beckoned to me, and put her arm around me. Basilisa brought her spindle and sat down on the floor next to the sofa. I heard my mother's teeth chattering. Basilisa rose to her knees and looked at her. My mother moaned:

"Drive out that cat scratching there under the sofa!"

Basilisa stooped down: "Where is the cat? I don't see it!"

"And you can't hear it either?"

The old woman, poking and probing with her spindle, replied:

"I can't hear it either!"

My mother screamed: "Antonia! Antonia!"

"Yes, ma'am?"

"What are you thinking about?"

"Nothing, ma'am."

"Don't you hear the cat scratching?"

Antonia listened for a moment: "It isn't scratching any more."

My mother trembled all over: "It's scratching right here in front of my feet, but I can't see it either!"

Her fingers were clenching my shoulders. Basilisa tried to bring a light over, but a gust of wind that rattled all the doors blew it out in her hand. Then, while our mother screamed and clutched my sister by the hair, the old woman took an olive branch dipped in holy water and began to sprinkle all the corners of the room.

14

My mother went to her bedroom. She rang the bell, and Basilisa hurried to her. Then Antonia opened the balcony window and looked out at the plaza with eyes that were half awake; she drew back slowly, and then hurried away. I was left alone, with my forehead pressed against the windowpane. Outside, the afternoon light was fading. I thought I heard screams deep within the house and I didn't dare move, sensing vaguely that those cries were something I shouldn't know about because I was only a child. I didn't budge from the window sill at the balcony; my head was buzzing with childish fears, mixed with a dim recollection of sharp scoldings and of being shut in a dark room. Those unhappy memories engulfed my soul, for I was one of those precocious children who leave off playing and listen wide-eyed to tales told by old women. Little by little the screaming stopped, and when all was quiet in the house I slipped out of the parlor. I met la Galinda coming out of one of the doors:

"Don't make any noise, you little rascal!"

On tiptoe, I stopped outside my mother's bedroom. Her door was ajar, and from within came a moan of pain and a strong smell of vinegar. Noiselessly I slipped inside the open door without moving it. My mother was lying in bed, with compresses on her forehead. The outline of her black-gloved hand stood out against the whiteness of the sheet. Her eyes were open, and as I entered she turned them toward the door without moving her head:

"My boy, chase away that cat there at my feet!"

I went over, and a black cat jumped down to the floor and ran out. Basilisa la Galinda, who was standing in the doorway, saw it, too, and said I had been able to frighten it away because I was pure at heart.

15

And I remember my mother sitting all during one long day in the dim light of a sunless room with its windows slightly open. She was whitefaced and motionless in her big chair, with her arms crossed upon her breast and handkerchief compresses upon her head. She did not speak, and when others talked she imposed silence by turning her eyes and gazing steadily at them. The clock meant nothing that day: it was all mid-afternoon shadows. But it ended abruptly as lights were brought into the bedroom. My mother was screaming:

"That cat! That cat! Get him off me! He's hanging down my back!"

Basilisa la Galinda came over to me, and with a great air of mystery pushed me toward my mother; then she bent down and whispered in my ear, her chin quivering and scratching my face with its hairy moles:

"Cross your hands!"

I crossed my hands, and Basilisa put them on my mother's back. Then, in a hushed voice she kept after me:

"What do you feel, child?"

Frightened, I answered in the same tone as the old woman:

"Nothing! I don't feel anything, Basilisa!"

"Don't you feel something like fire?"

"I feel nothing, Basilisa!"

"Can't you feel the cat's hairs?"

"Nothing."

And I burst into tears, frightened by my mother's screams. Basilisa picked me up and took me out into the hall.

"Oh, you little rascal, you have committed some sin; that's why you can't frighten away the Evil One!"

She went back into the bedroom. I stayed out in the hallway, filled with fear and anguish as I wondered about my childish sins. The screaming continued in the bedroom, and servants went all through the house with lights.

16

After that long, long day came a night just as long, with candles lighted before religious statues and conversations in a hushed voice outside doors that creaked as they were opened. I sat out in the hall near a table with a double candlestick on it, and began to think about the story of Goliath, the giant. Antonia, holding her handkerchief to her eyes, passed by and said to me in a ghost-like voice:

"What are you doing here?"

"Nothing."

"Why aren't you studying?"

I stared at her, astonished that she should ask me why I wasn't studying when our mother was ill. Antonia went on down the hallway, and I got to thinking again about that heathen giant who died of a blow with a stone. In those days I admired nothing so much as the skill with which the boy David handled his sling: I made up my mind to practice it the next time I took a walk along the river bank. I had some vague, wild idea of planting my shots on the pale forehead of the student Bretal.

Antonia went by again, carrying a small brazier for burning lavender:

"Why aren't you in bed, boy?"

And she hurried off down the hallway again. I didn't go to bed, but I did fall asleep with my head resting on the table.

17

I don't know whether it happened one night or many nights, because the house was always dark and candles were always burning before the religious images. I recall that in my sleep I kept hearing my mother's screams, the servants' mysterious whispering, the creaking of the doors, and the ringing of a bell outside in the street. Basilisa la Galinda would come for the candlestick, take it away for a moment, and bring it back with two new candles that gave scarcely any light. On one of these occasions, when I raised my head from the table I saw a man seated at the other side of it in his shirtsleeves, sewing. He was very small and balding, and wore a red waistcoat. He smiled a greeting:

"Were you asleep, my studious young fellow?"

Basilisa trimmed the candles:

"Don't you remember my brother, you little rascal?"

Struggling through the dim haze of sleep, I recalled Juan de Alberte. I had seen him some of those afternoons when the old woman took me up to the cathedral towers: Basilisa's brother used to mend cassocks in an attic room. La Galinda sighed:

"He is here to notify them when to come from the Chapel of Corticela to administer the last rites."

I started to cry, and the two old people told me not to make any noise. My mother could be heard screaming:

"Get that cat away from me! Get that cat away!"

Basilisa la Galinda went into the bedroom at the foot of the stairs that led to the garret, and came out with a black wooden cross. She mumbled some words indistinctly, and made the sign of the cross on my breast, my back, and my sides. Then she handed me the cross and picked up her brother's scissors, those big, rusty tailoring shears that opened with a metallic screak:

"We are going to free her, as she asks. . . ."

She led me by the hand into the bedroom, where my mother was still screaming:

"Get that cat away from me! Get that cat away from me!"

At the threshold she coached me, speaking softly:

"Go over very quietly and put the cross on the pillow. . . . I'll stay here at the door."

I went into the bedroom. My mother was sitting up, her hair all dishevelled, her hands extended, and her fingers curled like hooks. One hand was white, the other black. Antonia, pale and pleading, was staring at her. I circled around and looked straight at my sister: her eyes were sunken and had dark circles under them, but there were no tears. I got up on the bed quietly, and put the cross on the pillow. There at the door, hunched over the threshold, stood Basilisa la Galinda. I caught a glimpse of her for only a moment as I was climbing up on the bed, for no sooner had I put the cross on the pillow than my mother began to writhe: a black cat came out from among the covers and ran toward the door. I shut my eyes, and while they were closed I heard the click of Basilisa's scissors. Then the old woman came over to the bed where my mother was writhing, and carried me from the bedroom in her arms.

In the hall, near the table with the little tailor's shadow behind it, she showed me by the light of the candles two black patches that oozed blood on her hands: she said they were the cat's ears. The old man was putting on his cloak to summon the priest for the last rites.

18

The odor of candle wax and the confused murmur of people praying filled the house. . . . A priest in his vestments came in and hurried past, with one hand held to his lips. Guided by Juan de Alberte, he went through the doors. The tailor, stiff and dwarfish, paced up and down with his head turned to one side; with two fingers he kept twirling his cap by its visor, as artisans do in processions. After them came a slow and sombre group, praying softly, that walked down the middle of the corridor from one door to another in a solid line; some of the dark forms knelt in the hallway, and individuals became more distinguishable. They made a long line that stretched as far as the open doors of my mother's bedroom. Inside, Antonia and la Galinda were on their knees; they wore mantillas, and each held a candle in her hand. I kept being pushed forward by hands that stretched out from long, dark cloaks and quickly joined again around the crosses of their rosaries: they were the gnarled hands of old women who were praying in the hallway, lined up along the wall with their sharply etched shadows close to their bodies. In my mother's bedroom a woman was crying: she held a perfumed handkerchief, and in her Nazarene religious habit she looked to me like a large purple dahlia. She took my hand and knelt down with me, helping me to hold a candle. The priest walked around the bed, murmuring in Latin as he read from his prayer book. . . .

Then they raised the covers and revealed my mother's feet, rigid and yellowish. I understood that she was dead, and stood there silent and horrified in the warm arms of that lovely lady who was all purple and white. Too terror-stricken to cry out, I felt a frozen fear, a strange emptiness, and a strong reluctance to leave the arms and bosom of that white and purple lady whose cheek was lowered next to mine as she helped me hold the funeral candle.

19

La Galinda came and led me from the lady's arms over to the edge of the bed where my mother lay, rigid and yellowish, with her hands tucked between the folds of the sheet. Basilisa lifted me from the floor so I could get a clear view of that wax-like face:

"Say good-bye to her child. Tell her: 'Good-bye, mother dear, I won't see you any more.'"

The old woman put me down on the floor because she was growing tired; when she had caught her breath she lifted me up again by placing her gnarled hands beneath my arms:

"Take a good look at her so you'll remember her when you're grown up. . . . Kiss her, child."

She held me over the dead face. Almost brushing against those motionless eyelids, I began to scream and squirm in la Galinda's arms. Suddenly Antonia, with her hair down, appeared at the other side of the bed. She snatched me from the old servant's arms and pressed me to her bosom, sobbing and choking. My sister's anguished kisses, and the sight of her reddened eyes, distressed me deeply. . . . Antonia stood there motionless, and her face wore a strange expression of grief and determination. We went into another room, where she sat down on a low chair and took me on her lap: she caressed me, and kissed me again, sobbing. Then she began to wring my hands in hers, and to laugh and laugh and laugh. . . . One lady fanned her with her handkerchief; another, with frightened eyes, opened a bottle of smelling salts; another came in through the door with a glass of water that rattled on the metal tray.

20

I was standing in a corner, overwhelmed by a bewildering grief that made my temples throb painfully, as if I were seasick. I cried at times, and at times I stopped to listen to the weeping of the others. It must have been about midnight when the bedroom door was opened wide: I could see by the light of four candles flickering inside that my mother was laid out in her black coffin. I went in noiselessly and sat down on the window sill. Around the coffin three women and Basilisa's brother were keeping vigil. From time to time the tailor would rise and moisten his fingers to trim the candles. That spruce, dwarf-like tailor in his scarlet waistcoat had an indescribably clownish grace about him as he pinched off the wicks and puffed out his cheeks to spit on his fingers.

As I listened to the women's stories I gradually stopped crying: they were tales of ghosts, and of people buried alive.

21

As dawn was breaking, a very tall lady with dark eyes and white hair came into the room. She kissed my mother on her half-shut eyelids without shrinking from the chill of death, and almost without a tear. Then, kneeling down between two tapers, she moistened an olive branch in holy water and shook it over the corpse. Basilisa came in and looked around for me; raising her hand, she beckoned:

"Look at your grandmother, you little rascal!"

It was my grandmother! She had ridden in on a mule from her house in the hills, seven leagues from Santiago. At that moment I heard hoofs stamping on the stones in the yard where the mule had been tied. It was a sound that seemed to echo through the emptiness of the mournful house. From the doorway my sister Antonia called to me:

"Brother! Brother!"

At the old servant's urging, I went over very slowly. Antonia took me by the hand and led me into a corner:

"That lady is our grandmother. From now on we shall live with her."

I sighed: "Then why doesn't she kiss me?"

Antonia stood thinking a moment as she wiped her eyes:

"Foolish child! First she has to pray for Mamma!"

She prayed a long time. Finally she rose and asked for us. Antonia pulled me over by the hand. Our grandmother was now wearing a mourning kerchief over her curly, silver hair, which seemed to accentuate the brightness of her dark eyes. Her fingers brushed lightly across my cheek, and I still remember the impression produced upon me by that peasant hand: it was rough, and there was no tenderness in its touch. She spoke to us in the Galician dialect:

"Your mother's died, she has, and now 'tis I who'll be a mother to ye. Ye have no one to turn to in this world. . . . 'Tis comin' with me ye are, for this house is bein' closed. . . . Tomorrow, after Mass, we'll be startin' on our way."

22

The next day my grandmother closed up the house, and we started out for San Clemente de Brandeso. I was already out in the street and up on the mule of a hill-country man who was giving me a ride in front of him. Inside the house I heard the slamming of doors and the shouts of servants looking for my sister Antonia: they could not find her. With frightened faces they would come out on the balconies, go inside again, and run through the empty house, where the wind kept slamming the doors and voices kept calling my sister.

From the entrance to the cathedral a pious old woman spied her lying in a faint on our tiled roof. We called her and she opened her eyes to the morning sun, as frightened as though she were awakening from a bad dream. A sexton in shirtsleeves and cassock brought out a long ladder to get her down from the roof.

As we started away, the student Bretal appeared in the courtyard, his cape whipping in the wind. On his face he wore a dark bandage, and beneath it I thought I could see bloody gashes as if his ears had been cut off close to his head. . . .

23

Santiago de Galicia was once one of the world's shrines, and people there still keep their eyes ever alert for miracles.

Doña Emilia Pardo Bazán (1851–1921)

. . . was one of the most forceful Spanish novelists of the nineteenth century, and modern Spain's most outstanding woman writer. A child prodigy, she could read and write with ease at the age of four, composed poetry at eight, and at fourteen wrote penetrating critical essays on such classics of world literature as *The Divine Comedy* and *The Iliad.* In later life the title of Countess was conferred upon her because of the renown she had brought to her country; and so broad was her knowledge of European letters that a chair of Romance Literatures was created for her at the University of Madrid—the first professorship to be held by a woman in Spain.

After her youth, which she spent in her family's aristocratic manor house in Galicia, she married and went to live in Madrid and Paris. The young matron was vivacious and dynamic—overwhelming might be a more appropriate word—but not an attractive woman. After a few years she left her husband, settled in Madrid, and devoted herself to literature.

Doña Emilia was forceful—even virile—in her writing, as she was in her direct dealings with people. Her best novels describe life in her native region, but we find in them none of the wistful, Celtic charm of Galicia; only the misty-green landscape is described in all its dewy softness: the people—particularly the old aristocracy living in mouldering manor houses—are depicted as harsh, impoverished, and decadent. Her masterpiece in the field of the regional novel is *The Mansions of Ulloa* (1886). Together with its sequel, *Mother Nature* (1887), the story will remind English-speaking readers of Emily Brontë's *Wuthering Heights* in its stark, tragic—even repellent—picture of passion, greed and violence. Her writing at times involved Doña Emilia in trouble with the Church, but she herself was conservative and religious.

In addition to her work as a novelist, Pardo Bazán wrote splendid works of literary criticism. It was she who introduced Naturalism into Spain with her studies on Zola and the Russian novel. The Countess was also a dramatist, poetess, and a prolific writer of short stories. These have been gathered and published in eight volumes, and all are of high quality. It has been difficult, therefore, to choose one for this collection, but *The Talisman* is universally classified as among her very best.

The Talisman

THIS STORY, which is a true one, cannot be read in broad daylight. I advise you, reader, to turn on artificial light—not electricity or gas, or even a kerosene lamp, but one of those old-fashioned oil lamps that give only a faint light and leave most of the room in shadows. Or better yet: turn on no light at all; go out into the garden, and near the fountain where magnolias give off their heady fragrance and moonlight floods down in silvery beams, listen to the tale of Baron Helynagy and the mandrake.

I met the foreign gentleman (and I do not say this to lend an aura of truth to the tale, but because I really did meet him) in the simplest, most ordinary way in the world: he was introduced to me at one of the many parties given by the Austrian ambassador. The Baron was First Secretary of the Embassy, but neither his position nor his appearance nor his conversation— much like that of the majority of the people one meets —really called for the tone of mystery and the hesitant phrases with which I was informed that he would be introduced to me. It was as if they were announcing some important event.

My curiosity aroused, I proposed to observe the Baron carefully. He seemed very refined, with the refinement which is characteristic of diplomats, and handsome, with the somewhat stereotyped good looks of a typical well-groomed gentleman. As for the Baron's character and intellectual worth, it was hard for me to make a judgment in such ordinary surroundings. After a half hour's conversation I thought to myself once more, "I simply don't understand why they consider this man so remarkable."

Immediately after my chat with the Baron I began asking questions of everyone, and what I found out increased my lively interest in him. They told me that the Baron carried a talisman, no less. Yes, a real talisman: something that enabled him to carry out all his wishes and to be successful in everything he undertook. They told me about inexplicable strokes of luck attributable only to the magic influence of the talisman.

The Baron was a Hungarian, the last male member of the Helynagy family; and though he took pride in being a descendant of Taksony, the famous Magyar leader, the fact is that he was living in poverty in the old ancestral mansion in the mountains. Suddenly a series of rare coincidences dropped a considerable fortune into his lap: not only did several rich relatives die quite opportunely, leaving him their sole heir, but while repairs were being made in the ancient Helynagy castle a treasure in jewels and coins was discovered.

The Baron then presented himself at Court in Vienna, as befitted his rank, and there new signs were seen that only some mysterious protection could furnish the key to such extraordinary good fortune. If the Baron gambled, he was certain to win everyone's money; if he looked at a lady, it was a foregone conclusion that she would be receptive to his attentions. He fought three duels, and in all three he wounded his adversary; the third man died of his wound, and this was taken as Destiny's warning to the Baron's rivals in future. When he felt like entertaining political ambitions, the doors of Parliament opened wide for him; and his present post as Secretary of the Embassy in Madrid was simply a stepping-stone to higher honors. It was already being said that he would be named Minister Plenipotentiary next month.

Provided all of this was not a hoax, it was certainly worth my while to find out the sort of talisman with which one obtains such enviable results. I determined to investigate, because I have always worked on the principle that one should believe completely in the fantastic and the miraculous. One who does not believe —at least from eleven at night until five o'clock the next morning—is rather foolish.

To achieve my purpose I did exactly the opposite of what is usually done in such cases: I sought out the Baron and took every opportunity to speak to him frankly; but I never mentioned the talisman. Bored, probably, with amorous conquests, the Baron was quite willing to be a friend—nothing more—to a woman who treated him with cordial frankness. Nevertheless, for some time my strategy had no effect at all. What I discovered in the Baron was not the devil-may-care cheerfulness of one favored by Fate, but a certain sadness and restlessness, a kind of brooding pessimism. On the other hand, his repeated references to other times— his obscure and humble past—and to the sudden rise in his fortunes, confirmed the stories that were current. The news that the Baron had been recalled to Vienna, and that his departure was imminent, caused me to lose hope of learning anything more.

I was thinking about all this one afternoon, when whom should they announce but the Baron. He was calling to say good-bye to me, no doubt, and was carrying in his hand an object that he placed on the nearest small table. Then he seated himself and looked around as if to make certain that we were alone. I felt deeply stirred, for with feminine intuition I quickly sensed that he was going to speak of the talisman.

"I am here," said the Baron, "to ask you, madam, to do me a favor of inestimable value. You already know that I have been called to my homeland, and I imagine that my absence will be a short one. I have something . . . a kind of relic . . . and I fear that the hazards of the journey. . . . In short, I fear it may be stolen from me, for it is highly coveted and many people attribute astonishing powers to it. My trip has been publicized, and it is even quite possible that some plot may be afoot to rob me of this object. I am entrusting it to you; keep it for me until I return, and I shall be truly grateful to you."

So the precious talisman was right here, two feet from me, on top of a piece of my furniture, and was going to be placed in my hands!

"You may rest assured," I replied vehemently, "that if I keep it for you it will be well protected. But before accepting custody of it I should like you to inform me what it is that I am going to protect. Although I have never asked you any indiscreet questions, I am aware of what is being said, and I understand that you possess a prodigious talisman that has brought you all kinds of good fortune. I will not keep it without knowing what it is, and if it really merits such great interest."

The Baron hesitated. I saw that he was debating within himself before speaking with complete truth and frankness. Finally sincerity prevailed, and not without some effort he replied:

"You have touched, madam, upon the one great grief

in my heart. The constant burden of my life is my
doubt as to whether I really possess a treasure with
magic properties, or whether I am keeping, through
superstition, some worthless fetish. Belief in the supernatural is always, in these modern times, like a tower
with no firm foundation: the slightest puff of wind
topples it to the ground. People believe I am 'fortunate'
when in reality I am just 'lucky'; I would be happy if I
were completely certain that what is enclosed in this
box is, indeed, a talisman that makes my dreams come
true and wards off the blows of fate. But this is precisely
the point I am unable to verify.

"What can I possibly tell you? I was poor and un-
noticed by anybody, when one afternoon an Israelite on
his way from Palestine passed through Helynagy and
insisted upon selling me this thing, assuring me that it
would bring me all kinds of happiness. I bought it . . .
the way one buys a thousand useless things . . . and
put it into a box. In a short time things began to happen
that changed my luck. But all of them have an explanation . . . without the need of miracles."

Here the Baron smiled, and his smile was contagious.
Then his melancholy expression returned, and he continued:

"Every day we see men succeeding in fields where
they do not deserve it . . . unskilled duellists quite
often defeat famous swordsmen. If I were convinced
that talismen really exist, I would enjoy my prosperity
in peace. What embitters me is the thought that I may
be the victim of some cruel self-deception, and that
when I least expect it the sad fate of my race may over-
take me. Look how those who envy me are already
doing me harm, and how this tormenting fear of the
future is clouding my happiness! Even so, I still have

enough faith left to beg you to guard the box well for me . . . because the greatest misfortune a man can have is to be neither a complete skeptic nor a devout believer."

This frank confession explained the sadness I had noted on the Baron's face. His spiritual situation seemed pathetic to me, for amid the greatest good fortune lack of faith was gnawing at his soul. The masterful haughtiness of great men always comes from firm belief in their destiny, and Baron Helynagy, incapable of this belief, was incapable of winning through to success.

The Baron rose, and picking up the object he had brought, he unfolded the black silk cloth in which it was wrapped. I saw a little crystal box with a silver lock. When the cover was raised I beheld upon a linen shroud which the Baron delicately unwound a horrid thing: a blackish, grotesque little figure that looked like the body of a man. My gesture of repugnance did not surprise the Baron.

"But . . . what is it?" I forced myself to ask him.

"This," replied the diplomat, "is one of the marvels of Nature. It is not a carving or an imitation; it is a genuine root of the mandrake plant, exactly as it grows beneath the earth. The superstition that attributes weird powers to the mandrake root is as old as the world itself. They say it grows from the blood of people who have been executed, and that for this reason the mandrake can be heard moaning in the middle of the night as if some soul dwelt captive within it, sunk in deep despair. Ah! Be careful, for the love of Heaven, to keep it wrapped constantly in a silk or linen shroud; only in this way does the mandrake afford its protection."

"And you believe all this?" I exclaimed, eyeing the Baron steadily.

"Would that I did!" he answered in a tone so bitter that at first I could find no words in reply.

In a short while the Baron said good-bye, and he repeated his admonition that I should be very careful of the box and its contents—just in case anything should happen. He stated that he expected to return within a month, and that he would pick up the box at that time.

As soon as the talisman came into my custody, you may be sure that I examined it more closely. I confess that although the whole legend of the mandrake seemed to me a crude hoax and an evil superstition from the Orient, I could not but be impressed by the rare perfection with which that root resembled the human body. I thought it must be some clever imitation, but careful inspection convinced me that the hand of man had no part in the freakish thing; it was a natural phenomenon, the root itself just as it had been pulled from the ground. I asked several people who had lived for a long time in Palestine; they assured me that it is not possible to counterfeit a mandrake, and that it is plucked and sold just that way by shepherds in the hills of Gilead and on the plains of Jericho.

No doubt the strangeness of the object, completely unfamiliar to me, was what excited my imagination. The fact of the matter is that I began to be afraid, or at least to feel an uncontrollable revulsion toward the accursed talisman. I had put it away with my jewels inside the safe in my bedroom. The slightest noise would awaken me trembling, and sometimes the wind rattling the window panes and rustling the curtains made me imagine that the mandrake was sobbing with unearthly cries. . . .

In short, there was no living with the horrid thing, and I decided to take it out of my room and put it into a glass cabinet in the living room where I kept rare coins and medallions. This act was the source of my everlasting sorrow, which will never leave me as long as I live.

Fate so willed it that a new servant, tempted by the coins in the cabinet, broke the glass in order to steal them, and at the same time carried off the little box with the talisman.

It was a terrible blow to me. I notified the police who moved heaven and earth. The thief was found . . . yes, found; the coins were recovered, along with the little box and the winding cloth . . . but the man confessed that he had thrown the talisman into a sewer. It was nowhere to be found, even at the cost of the most expensive investigations imaginable.

"And Baron Helynagy?" I asked the lady who had told me this singular story.

"He died in a railroad accident on the way back to Spain," she answered, turning away her face, which had grown paler than usual.

"So that was indeed a real talisman. . . . ?"

"Good Heavens!" she replied. "Don't you believe at all in coincidences?"

Leopoldo Alas (1852–1901)

. . . came from Asturias on the north coast of Spain, where the Cantabrian Mountains plunge down to the Bay of Biscay. The hardy fisherfolk and rugged miners of this region are proud of the fact that their province is called "the cradle of the Spanish race": it was the only part of the peninsula never conquered by the Moors, and from here the reconquest of Spain from the invaders began under the first Spanish king, Pelayo, in 718.

This bristling spirit of independence is fully evident in Leopoldo Alas, who wrote under the name "Clarín"—the war trumpet. He was the most scathing critic of the social and political system in Spain at the end of the nineteenth century, and inspired many of the angry young men of the reformist Generation of 1898. Professor of Law and Political Science at the University of Oviedo, his alma mater, he was the forerunner of others in academic life who were to be vigorous critics of the status quo in the first three decades of the twentieth century.

"Clarín" was a splendid literary critic of prose and poetry, and wrote the best contemporary analysis of Spain's outstanding nineteenth-century novelist, Pérez Galdós. He was also a novelist in his own right: his best, a two-volume work entitled *The Regent's Wife* (1884–1885), is one of the finest of the realist-naturalist genre in Spain. It is a pitiless probe into middle-class life in a dull provincial capital—obviously Oviedo itself—and is written with subtle irony and finely-drawn characterizations. His analysis of the protagonist, Ana Ozores, caught in a mystical-sensual conflict, is a profound psychological study of an adulteress who strangely fascinates a clergyman at the cathedral. In this searching, searing study, "Clarín," who knew Oviedo like the palm of his hand (he never left it except for brief stays in Madrid), has written one of the masterpieces of the nineteenth-century Spanish novel.

In his many short stories he strikes a lighter note, but quite a few are critical of the established order. The story translated in this present collection, *Adiós, Cordera!*, has become a classic tale of the universal Spanish conflict between the *patria chica*—one's own small province—and the *patria grande*, Spain itself. This strong regionalism, tinged with deep disenchantment about the modernization of Spain, is nowhere better expressed than in the following simple story.

Adiós, Cordera!

THERE WERE three of them—always the three of them: Rosa, Pinín, and Cordera.

The Somonte meadow was a three-cornered patch of green velvet that stretched like a tapestry down the slope of a long, low hill. One of its corners, the lowest one, was cut off by the railroad that ran from Oviedo to Gijón. A telegraph pole, with its white insulators and parallel wires on either side, stood there like a conqueror's banner; for Rosa and Pinín it represented the big, outside world of which they knew nothing—mysterious, terrible, forever unknown. After considering the matter carefully, and after many days of looking at the pole—quiet, inoffensive, good-humored, desirous no doubt of acclimating itself to the village and looking as much as possible like a dry tree—Pinín grew bolder and carried his confidence to the point of putting his arms around the wood and climbing up toward the wires. But he never touched the porcelain insulators up there; they reminded him of the chocolate cups he had seen in the rectory at Puno. When he found himself so near the sacred mystery, he would be seized by a panicky respect and let himself slide down quickly until he felt his feet upon the turf.

Rosa, less daring, but more fascinated by the unknown, would content herself with putting her ear next to the telegraph pole and would spend many minutes—a quarter of an hour at a time—listening to the awe-inspiring metallic sounds that came down the dry pine wood as the wires vibrated in the wind. Those vibrations, at times intense like those of a tuning fork that seems to burn the ear with its giddy throb if placed too close, were for Rosa messages that were going through the wires, letters written in an incomprehensible language, the unknown speaking to the unknown. She was not burning with curiosity to understand what the people so far away off there were saying to those other people on the opposite side of the world. What difference did it make to her? Her interest was in the sound for its own sake—its timbre and its mystery.

Cordera, much more formal than her companions (although, to be sure, she was of a much greater age) abstained from all communication with the world of men, and looked upon the telegraph pole as what it was, indeed, for her: a dead, useless thing which was not even useful to her for scratching herself. She was a cow who had lived a long time. Just sitting there hour after hour, and skilled in choosing pasture grass, she knew how to employ her time. She did more thinking than eating, and she enjoyed the pleasure of living in peace beneath the calm, grey sky of her native heath, just like a person refreshing his soul—for animals have souls, too. And if it were not disrespectful we might say that the thoughts of the old cow, who had had much experience, must have seemed a lot like the most peaceful, philosophical odes of Horace.

Like a grandmother she watched the games of the two little ones whose duty it was to take her out to pasture. Had she been able to, she would have smiled at the thought that Rosa and Pinín were charged with seeing to it that she, Cordera, did not wander off, or walk on the railroad tracks, or jump over the fence into the next field. As if she would jump! As if she would stray!

To graze a little from time to time, each day less, without wasting time to raise her head in foolish curiosity, choosing unhesitatingly the best tufts of grass, and then to settle down comfortably on her hind quarters and think about life, enjoying the pleasure of not working hard and just letting life roll by—this was all she had to do; everything else was a dangerous adventure. She no longer even remembered when a fly had bitten her. The *xatu*—the bull—and crazy runs through the meadow . . . all of that was so far back!

That peaceful existence had been disturbed only during the days of the inauguration of the new railroad. The first time Cordera saw the train go by she went crazy: she jumped the fence at the top of Somonte meadow and ran through other farmers' fields. The fright lasted several days, and was renewed, on a greater or lesser scale, whenever the engine came through the nearby railroad cut. When she finally realized that it was a fleeting danger, a catastrophe that threatened but never struck, she reduced her precautions to rising to her feet, raising her head, and looking straight at the formidable monster. Later she did not rise but merely looked at it with loathing and mistrust. Finally she did not even bother to look at the train.

On Pinín and Rosa the novelty of the railroad produced more agreeable and lasting impressions. If at first it was a mad joy somewhat mixed with awestruck fear, a nervous excitement that caused them to burst into shouts, gestures, and wild grimaces, later it became a gentle, peaceful entertainment that was repeated several times each day. It took a long time for that thrill to wear off: the train flew by like some long, iron dragon amid a giddy rush of wind and so much noise, and inside of it there were so many kinds of strange, unknown people.

But the telegraph, the railroad, all of that, was extremely unimportant—just a passing event drowned in the sea of solitude that surrounded the Somonte meadow; from there no human habitation could be seen, and no noises reached it from the outside world except when the train went by.

Through the long mornings, beneath the rays of the sun as it broke through the clouds, and amid the buzzing of the insects, the cow and the children would wait until noontime to go home for lunch. And then the endless afternoons of sweet, melancholy silence in the same meadow until nightfall, with the evening star as a mute witness on high. The clouds scudded by above, the shadows of the trees and rocks grew longer on the hill and in the glen, the birds sought their nests, some stars would begin to shine in the darkest patches of the blue sky, and the twins, Pinín and Rosa, children of Antón de Chinta, their souls tinged with the sweet, sleepy serenity of Nature in her solemn seriousness, would be still for hours on end after their games, which were never very noisy, seated near Cordera, who would accompany the august silence from time to time with the soft, lazy clanking of her cowbell.

In all this silence, in this calm inactivity, there was love. The brother and sister were as close to each other as the two halves of a piece of fruit, united by the same life and scarcely conscious of the many differences between them. Pinín and Rosa loved Cordera, the grandmother cow, big and yellowish, whose neck was like a cradle to them. Cordera would probably remind a poet of the *zavala*, the sacred cow of Ramayana; she had, in the fullness of her form and the solemn serenity of her slow and noble movements, the air and appearance of a fallen and forgotten idol, content with her lot, happier to be a real cow than a false god. It might be said that Cordera—as far as we can speculate about such things —also loved the twins who were in charge of taking her out to pasture. She could not express herself, but the patience she showed toward them when the children used her as a pillow, a hiding-place, a saddle, and other things that occurred to them in their games, revealed better than words the affection of the peaceful, pensive animal.

When times were hard, Pinín and Rosa had shown the greatest solicitude and done the impossible for Cordera. Antón de Chinta had not always owned the Somonte meadow: this pleasure was relatively new. Years before, Cordera had had to go out on her own, that is, to graze as best she could along the paths and byways of the scanty, close-cropped public meadow-lands, which were as much a thoroughfare as a pasture. Pinín and Rosa, in those days of poverty, used to lead her to the best knolls, to the most unfrequented and least grazed spots, and would spare her the risks run by the poor cattle that have to forage for food along the highway.

In times of hunger, when hay was scarce in the stable and straw to make a warm bed for the cow was lacking, too, Cordera owed to Rosa and Pinín the thousand little attentions that made poverty more bearable. And what of the heroic times when a calf was born and had to be fed? There was an understandable struggle between the needs of the new-born and those of the Chinta family, which meant taking from the udders of the poor cow every bit of milk not absolutely necessary for raising the calf. Rosa and Pinín, in these difficult times, always favored Cordera, and whenever there was a chance they would secretly untie the calf, which ran blindly and bumping its head crazily into everything to seek the mother, who would shelter it beneath her belly and turn her head fondly and gratefully as if to say in her own way: "Suffer little children—and suckling calves —to come unto me."

These memories, these bonds, are the kind that are never forgotten.

Add to all this the fact that Cordera had the best disposition of any cow in the world. When she found herself teamed with any other cow beneath a yoke, she would yield to its pressure and surrender her will to another's; and hour after hour she could be seen with her neck bent and her head in an uncomfortable position as she stood there on guard while the two children slept on the ground.

*

Antón de Chinta realized that he was fated to be a poor man when he came to the conclusion that it would be impossible for him ever to fulfill that golden dream of his: to have a herd of his own with at least four cows. Thanks to a thousand rigorous economies—the result of a sea of sweat and a purgatory of privation— he finally acquired one cow, Cordera, and never went beyond that point. Before he could buy the second he found himself obliged, in order to pay arrears to the owner of the little farmhouse he rented, to take Cordera to market—Cordera, that bit of his own heart and the darling of his children.

His wife had died two years after their purchase of Cordera. The stable and the couple's bed were on opposite sides of the wall, if a network of chestnut branches and cornstalks can be called a wall. Chinta's wife, the muse of economy in that wretched household, had died with her eyes fixed on Cordera through a hole in the broken partition, calling the cow the family's salvation.

"Take care of her: she is your support," the eyes of the poor woman seemed to say as she lay dying of malnutrition and overwork.

The twins had then concentrated their love upon Cordera: the mother's lap, with its special affection that a father cannot replace, was now the warmth of the cow, in the stable and there in the Somonte meadow.

Antón understood all this in a somewhat hazy manner. There was no need to say a word to the children about the need to sell Cordera. One Saturday in July at the break of dawn Antón, all out of sorts, started walking toward Gijón with the cow ahead of him; she wore only the rope from which the cowbell usually hung. Rosa and Pinín were asleep; other days they had to be awakened forcibly. The father let them sleep peacefully, and when they got up they found Cordera missing.

"Without doubt, Papa has taken her to the bull."

There was no room for doubt. Rosa and Pinín were of the opinion that the cow was going unwillingly; they believed that she did not want any more calves, since she ended by losing them all very soon, without knowing how or when.

At nightfall Antón and Cordera came into the corral sad, tired, and covered with dust. The father gave them no explanation, but the children sensed the danger.

He had not sold her because no one had wanted to
meet the price he had taken it into his head to ask. It
was too high, dictated psychologically by his affection.
He had asked a lot for the cow so that no one would
attempt to take her. Those who had come over to try
their luck had soon gone away fuming at that man who
looked with a challenging, rancorous eye upon anyone
who insisted upon approaching the price behind which
he was taking refuge. Antón de Chinta had stayed at
the Humedal Market until closing time, giving fate a
chance.

"It cannot be said," he kept thinking, "that I don't
want to sell; they are the ones who won't pay me what
Cordera is worth."

And finally, with a sigh of consolation—if not of
satisfaction—he took up his march again along the
Candás highway, among all the confusion and noise
of pigs, oxen, cows and young bulls that the villagers
from many districts roundabout were having a difficult
or an easy time leading along, depending upon the
length of the relationship between owner and animal.

At Natahoyo, where two roads cross, Chinta still
might have sold Cordera. A farmer from Carrió who
had been bothering him all day, offering just a few
duros under what he was asking, accosted Chinta for
the last time. Slightly drunk, the farmer kept going up
and up in his bid, in a battle between his love of money
and his desire to get the cow. The two men reached the
point in their bargaining where each took the other's
hands, standing there in the middle of the road blocking
the way . . . but finally greed won out; the small
amount of fifty *pesetas* separated them like an abyss.
They let go of one another's hands, and each went his
own way. Antón took a path which wound between

honeysuckle not yet in flower and blackberry bushes in bloom, and finally reached home.

*

From that day when they sensed the danger, Pinín and Rosa knew no rest. The middle of the week following, the overseer appeared at Antón's corral; he was another villager from the same district, an irascible man who was hard with tenants in arrears. Antón, who was not the kind of man to stand for reprimands, became livid at the threat of eviction.

The owner would wait no more? All right! He would sell the cow at a miserable price—for a song. He had to pay up, or be dispossessed.

The next Saturday Pinín accompanied his father to the Humedal Market. The boy looked at the meat dealers with horror: they were the tyrants of the market place. Cordera was bought at a reasonable price by the highest bidder, who was from Castile. A mark was made on her hide to show she had been sold and belonged now to someone else. She returned to her stable, her bell clanking sadly; behind her came Antón de Chinta walking along in silence, and Pinín with eyes as big as saucers.

When Rosa learned of the sale she hugged the neck of Cordera, who lowered her head to be caressed as she did to be yoked.

"The old cow is going!" thought the shy Antón, broken-hearted. She as a living creature was only an animal, but his children had no other mother or grandmother.

During those next days in the green Somonte pasture the silence was funereal. Cordera, ignorant of her fate, rested and grazed as always *sub specie aeternitatis*, just as she would be resting and chewing a minute before the brutal blow would knock her dead. But Pinín and Rosa lay there sick at heart, stretched out on the grass which would be unused from then on. With hatred they looked at the telegraph wires and the trains that went by. It was that unknown world, far away in all directions, that was taking their Cordera from them.

On Friday evening came the farewell. An employe of the Castilian buyer arrived for the cow. He paid; Antón and the man had a drink, and Cordera was brought out.

Antón had emptied the bottle, and was excited; the weight of the money in his pocket was stimulating, too. He wanted to dull his grief, and spoke at length, praising the cow's good qualities. The man smiled, because Antón's praises were useless. So the cow gave this many quarts of milk? So she was patient when yoked, and strong when pulling? What difference did it make, when in a few days she was going to be cut up into chops and other delicious morsels? Antón did not want to think of this; he kept imagining her as alive, working for another farmer, forgotten by him and his children—but alive and happy.

Pinín and Rosa, seated upon a pile of hay which was for them a sentimental reminder of Cordera and their own duties, were holding one another by the hand and looking at their enemy with frightened eyes. At the last moment they threw themselves upon their friend with kisses, embraces, everything. They could not tear themselves away. Antón, the stimulus of the wine suddenly gone, fell into a deep depression; he folded his arms and went into the dark corral.

For quite a distance along the hedge-bordered lane the children sadly followed the indifferent employe and their Cordera, who was going along unwillingly with someone strange at such an hour. Finally they had to leave her. Antón was shouting ill-humoredly from the house:

"Bah, children! Come here, I tell you! That's enough foolishness!"

That is what the father was calling from afar, but there were tears in his voice.

Night closed in. Down the dark lane, made almost black by the shadows of the high hedges, which nearly met overhead, forming an arch, the dark form of Cordera was lost in the distance. After that, there was only the slow, far-away clanking of her cowbell growing fainter amid the mournful chirping of myriad locusts.

"Adiós, Cordera!" Rosa cried, dissolved in tears. "Adiós, my darling Cordera!"

"Adiós, Cordera!" Pinín repeated, just as emotionally.

"Adiós," the cowbell answered in its own way. And its sad, submissive lament merged with the other rustic sounds of the July evening. . . .

*

The following day, very early, Pinín and Rosa went to the Somonte meadow as usual. Somonte's solitude had never seemed sad to them, but that day without Cordera it seemed a desert wasteland.

Suddenly the engine whistled; they saw the smoke, and then the train. In a freight car, through some narrow openings for ventilation, the twins glimpsed the heads of frightened cattle looking out between the spaces.

"Adiós, Cordera!" cried Rosa, guessing that her friend, the grandmother cow, was in there.

"Adiós, Cordera!" shouted Pinín, who believed it, too, shaking his fist at the train that went speeding toward Castile.

More aware than his sister of the wickedness of the world, the boy kept repeating through his tears:

"They're taking her to the slaughter house . . . to feed her to the rich, and to the priests. . . ."

"Adiós, Cordera!"

"Adiós, Cordera!"

Rosa and Pinín looked with hatred at the tracks and the telegraph, symbols of the enemy world which was taking away and destroying the companion of all their many days of sweet, silent solitude . . . to make succulent morsels for rich gluttons. . . .

"Adiós, Cordera!"

"Adiós, Cordera!"

*

Many years went by. Pinín grew up to be a young man, and the king took him away. The Carlist War was raging. Antón de Chinta was a tenant of one of the defeated politicians: there was no influence to get an exemption for Pinín, who was as strong as an oak.

And one grey October afternoon Rosa, all alone in the Somonte meadow, waited for the mail train from Gijón to pass. It was taking away her only love—her brother. The engine whistled in the distance, the train appeared in the railroad cut, and passed by with lightning speed. Rosa, very close to the tracks, could see for a moment in a third-class coach the heads of many poor recruits who were shouting, gesticulating, and saying farewell to the trees, the earth, the fields, the familiar countryside—their own little country—which they were leaving in order to go and die in the fratricidal struggles of the big country, for a king they did not know and ideas they did not understand.

Pinín, his body half out of a window, stretched his arms toward his sister: they almost touched. And Rosa could hear her brother distinctly, amid the noise of the wheels and the shouts of the recruits, with a sob in his voice as he exclaimed, moved by a remembered grief:

"Adiós, Rosa! Adiós, Cordera!"

"Adiós, Pinín! Adiós, my darling Pinín!"

There he went, just like her other love, the grandmother cow. The world was taking him away. The cow's flesh went to feed rich gluttons; his flesh was going to be cannon fodder for the world's madness, for other people's ambitions.

Such was the welter of ideas that teemed through the poor sister's mind as she watched the train fade away in the distance, its mournful whistle echoing among the trees, the fields, and the rocky hills . . . How alone she was! Now indeed—now indeed—the Somonte meadow was a desert wasteland.

"Adiós, Pinín! Adiós, Cordera!"

With what hatred Rosa looked at the track and its cinders, and with what wrath at the telegraph wires! How right Cordera was not to go near them! That was the unknown, outside world that carried everything off. And without thinking, Rosa rested her head against the pole that stood there like a conqueror's banner in the corner of the Somonte meadow. The wind hummed its metallic song inside the dry pine post. Now at last Rosa understood: it was a song of tears, of desolation, of loneliness, of death. And in its rapid, plaintive vibrations she thought she could hear—very far away—a voice that went sobbing along the track ahead:

"Adiós, Rosa! Adiós, Cordera!"

Armando Palacio Valdés (1853–1938)

. . . was, like his friend "Clarín," an Asturian. These two contemporaries (Alas was born in 1852) collaborated in at least one fine volume of literary criticism. But while Alas went into academic life, Palacio Valdés, after studying law at the University of Madrid, remained in the capital and in 1876 became director of the most influential literary review in Spain in those times, the *Revista Europea*. He had independent means, and remained aloof from the literary groups of his day; perhaps that is why the Spanish press paid little tribute to him. He was very popular abroad, however: for example, one of his sentimental novels, *Maximina*, sold over two hundred thousand copies in England, and in the United States his works have long been widely read and studied by students of Spanish in schools and colleges.

Palacio Valdés presents regional life with lightness, charm, humor and optimism, thus striking a note quite different from that of his fellow Asturian, "Clarín." He even wrote on regions other than his own. For instance, his most sparkling and delightful novel is *Sister San Sulpicio* (1889), written in the first person by a young Galician doctor who goes to Seville to convince a novice nun not to take her final vows but to marry him instead. It is one of the most colorful books ever written about Seville, with its bullfights, flamenco dancers, and Andalusian gaiety. We are all the more captivated because we see it through the eyes of a non-Andalusian like ourselves, and discover Seville's charms along with the newly-arrived doctor.

The region of Valencia, on the sunny Mediterranean coast, is portrayed by Palacio Valdés in *The Joy of Captain Ribot* (1899), a wholesome work about a sea captain and his enduring love. But maritime life is best captured in his regional novel *José* (1885), whose background is his own rugged Asturias, where the mountains drop down sheer to the sea. It describes the life of the hardy Asturian fisherfolk on the storm-tossed Bay of Biscay. *Martha and Mary* (1883) is another fine novel with an Asturian background, against which is set a moving story of the conflict between mysticism and worldly love.

In his short stories Palacio Valdés' good humor, optimism and abiding faith in humanity are clearly evident. The following selection, known and loved throughout the Spanish-speaking world, is a case in point.

Polyphemus

COLONEL TOLEDANO, nicknamed Polyphemus, was a fierce-looking man who wore a long frock coat, checkered trousers, and a high hat with a wide, curled-up brim. He was a giant of a man with a stiff and stately stride, enormous white mustachios, a voice of thunder and a heart of bronze. But even more than all this, the grim and bloodthirsty look in his only eye struck fear and horror into our hearts.

The colonel had lost one eye in the African War, where he had killed many Moors and had taken pleasure in tearing out their still-quivering insides. At least that was the firm belief of all of us who used to play after school in the Parque de San Francisco in the very noble and heroic city of Oviedo. The dauntless warrior used to walk there methodically on clear days from twelve to two o'clock. From afar we could glimpse his haughty figure among the trees: it struck fear into our childish hearts. And even when we could not see him, we could hear his stentorian voice booming through the bushes like a plunging waterfall.

The colonel was also hard of hearing, and always shouted as he spoke. "I am going to tell you a secret," he would say to whoever was accompanying him on his walk. "My niece Jacinta does not want to marry the Navarrete boy." And everyone within a radius of two hundred paces would learn about the secret.

He usually walked alone, but when a friend came along he was happy to see him. Perhaps he willingly accepted company so as to have occasion to open the cavern where he kept his powerful voice imprisoned. In fact, while he had a listener the Parque de San Francisco would shake. It was no longer a public walk: it was virtually the colonel's private preserve. Everything fell silent—the warbling of the birds, the whisper of the wind, and the soft murmur of the fountains. The only sound was the stern, commanding, clipped voice of the veteran from Africa; in fact, it seemed that the clergyman who accompanied him (at that hour only a few clergymen went walking in the park) was there for the sole purpose of opening—one after another— all the registers of the colonel's voice. When we heard those terrifying, thundering shouts and saw his violent gestures and fiery eye, how often we thought that he was going to pounce upon the luckless priest who had been so reckless as to come near him!

This frightful man had a nephew who was eight or ten years old, like us. Poor boy! When we saw him walking there we could not help feeling deeply sorry for him. In my time I have watched a wild animal trainer put a lamb into a lion's cage; it gave me exactly the same feeling as seeing little Gaspar Toledano walking with his uncle. We didn't understand how that poor boy could keep his appetite and go on living normally, or why he didn't grow heartsick or die, consumed by a slow fever. If a few days passed and he did not appear in the park, the same doubt gnawed at the hearts of us all: "Can Polyphemus have eaten the boy for a snack?"

And when at last we found him safe and sound somewhere, we were pleased and astonished at the same time. But we were sure that one day he would end up being the victim of some bloodthirsty whim of Polyphemus.

The strange part of all this was that little Gaspar's bright face showed none of those signs of terror and dejection that should have been indelibly stamped upon it. Quite to the contrary, his eyes always glowed with a genial joy that amazed us. When he went with his uncle he would walk along completely at ease, smiling and happy. Sometimes he would skip along, and others he would walk quietly; his audacity even reached the point of making faces at us behind his uncle's back. It produced in us the same anguished sensation as if we were watching him dance on the weathervane atop the cathedral spire.

"Gaspar!"

The shattered air would transmit that roar to the ends of the promenade, and every one of us there would blanch. Only little Gaspar would heed the call, as if it were a siren's: "What is it, uncle?"

And executing some intricate dance step, he would prance off in its direction.

In addition to this nephew, the monster had a dog who must have lived in the same unhappy state, although it gave no appearance of doing so. It was a handsome Great Dane, slate-blue in color, huge, lithe and vigorous, who answered to the name of Muley—in remembrance, no doubt, of some unhappy Moor slaughtered by the dog's master. Muley, like little Gaspar, lived in the power of Polyphemus as if on the lap of an odalisque. Supple, playful, frisky, faithful and harmless, he was the least frightening and most friendly dog I ever knew in my life.

With these qualities, it was not surprising that all of

us boys loved him. Whenever it was possible to do so without danger of having the colonel notice it, we would contend for the privilege of giving him some bread, crackers, cheese, or other tidbits that our mothers gave us for snacks. Muley would accept it with real joy, and would clearly show us his affection and gratitude. But to show how noble and disinterested were the feelings of this memorable canine, so that he may serve as an enduring example to dogs and men, I shall say that his affection toward the giver did not depend upon the size of the gift. A poor little boy named Andrés from the orphan asylum used to play with us sometimes (back in those days in the provinces there were no social barriers among children), but he could give him nothing because he had nothing. It happened that Muley's preference was for him. The most vigorous tail-wagging, and the highest and liveliest jumps, were reserved for him, not for the others. What a lesson for any majority congressman!

Did Muley guess that that unfortunate boy, always so sad and silent, needed his affection more than we did? I do not know, but it seemed that way.

For his part, little Andrés had developed a real love for the animal. When we were playing quoits at the far end of the park and Muley suddenly appeared, it was a foregone conclusion that Andrés would go off to play with him for quite a while, as if he had some secret to share with him. And there through the trees we could glimpse the colossal silhouette of Polyphemus.

But these hurried, furtive visits began to seem too short for the orphan. Like a true lover, he longed to enjoy the company of his idol alone and for a long time. Therefore one afternoon, with incredible daring and right before our eyes, he took the dog away with him to the Hospice, as the orphan asylum is called in Oviedo, and didn't return until a whole hour had passed. He came back radiant with joy. Muley, too, seemed extremely happy. Fortunately, the colonel had not left the park or noticed the absence of his dog.

On successive afternoons these excursions were repeated, and the friendship of little Andrés and Muley grew stronger. The boy would not have hesitated to give his life for the dog, and I am sure that the latter would have done no less if the occasion had arisen. But the orphan was still not satisfied. There formed in his mind the idea of taking Muley with him to sleep overnight at the asylum. As a kitchen helper, Andrés slept in one of the corridors outside the cook's room on a makeshift mattress of cornstalks.

One afternoon he led the dog to the Hospice and did not return. What a delightful night for the poor child! He had never known affection in his life except from Muley. His teachers first, and then the cook, had always spoken to him with a whip in their hands. He and the dog slept curled up like two newlyweds. At dawn there, the boy felt a smarting pain where the cook had struck him with a stick the preceding afternoon. He took off his shirt.

"Look, Muley," he said softly, showing him the bruise. The dog, more compassionate than the man, licked the black-and-blue spot on his flesh.

As soon as the doors were opened he let the dog loose, and Muley ran to his master's house. But that afternoon he was in the park again, ready to follow little Andrés. They slept side by side again that night, and the next, and the next also. But joy is short-lived in this world: Andrés was being happy on the edge of an abyss.

One afternoon when we were all close together in a group playing buttons, we heard behind us two crackling explosions:

"Halt! Halt!"

All heads turned as if moved by a spring. Before us towered the Cyclopean mass of Colonel Toledano.

"Which of you is the rascal who steals my dog every night? Out with it!"

A sepulchral silence in the crowd. Terror held us transformed, rigid, as if we were wooden sticks. Again the trump of the Last Judgment rang out:

"Who is the thief? Who is the bandit? Who is the . . . the *wretch?*"

The fiery eye of Polyphemus consumed us all, one after another. Muley, who was with him, looked at us with his eyes, too—loyal, innocent—and he kept wagging his tail vigorously, revealing his restlessness.

Then little Andrés, whiter than wax, took one step forward and said:

"Don't blame anyone, sir. I was the one."

"What!"

"I was the one," the boy repeated in a louder voice.

"Oho! So it was you!" said the colonel, grinning fiercely. "And don't you know whose dog this is?"

Little Andrés kept silent.

"Don't you know whose he is?" he asked again, at the top of his voice.

"Yes, sir."

"What? Speak louder!" And he cupped his hand to his ear.

"Yes, sir."

"Well, out with it! Whose is he?"

"He belongs to Polyphemus."

I closed my eyes. I think my playmates must have

done the same. When I opened them I thought little Andrés would already have been erased from the book of life. Fortunately, it was not so. The colonel was looking at him steadily, with curiosity rather than anger.

"And just why do you take him away with you?"

"Because he is my friend and he loves me," said the boy in an unshaken voice.

The colonel looked at him steadily once again.

"All right," he said at length, "but be careful not to take him again! If you do, rest assured that I'll pull your ears off!"

And he spun majestically on his heels. But before taking a step he put his hand into his vest, took out a large coin, and said as he turned around:

"Here, get yourself some candy. But remember not to steal the dog again! Remember!"

He started off, but after four or five paces it occurred to him to turn his head. Little Andrés had let the coin fall to the ground, and with his hands over his face he stood sobbing. The colonel hurried back.

"Are you crying? Why? Don't cry, my boy!"

"I love him very much . . . and he is the only one in the world who loves me," sobbed Andrés.

"But whose child are you?" asked the colonel in surprise.

"I'm from the orphanage."

"What?" shouted Polyphemus.

"I am an orphan."

Then we saw the colonel change completely. He picked the boy up, took his hands from his face, wiped away his tears with a handkerchief, hugged and kissed him, and repeated brokenly:

"Forgive me, my boy, forgive me! Pay no attention to what I said. Take the dog whenever you wish. Keep him with you as long as you like. Understand? As long as you like. . . ."

And after he had comforted the boy with these and other words, spoken in a tone of voice we never suspected that he possessed, he continued his walk, turning time and again to shout back:

"You can take him with you whenever you wish. Understand, my boy? Whenever you wish. . . ."

May God forgive me, but I could have sworn I saw a tear in the ferocious eye of Polyphemus.

Little Andrés went running off followed by his friend, who was barking with joy.

Ramón Pérez de Ayala (1880–)

. . . is one of the greatest stylists of modern Spanish letters. Born in Asturias, he received his early schooling under the Jesuits; at the University of Oviedo he came under the influence of Leopoldo Alas ("Clarín") who was his professor in the Law School there; and later he became a friend and admirer of Galdós, Spain's greatest modern novelist. With all these influences it is not surprising the Pérez de Ayala's works are masterpieces of subtle irony, philosophical humor, and psychological penetration. His keen mind cuts through all pretense, and a caustic skepticism pervades most of his work.

Don Ramón is a cosmopolitan who has travelled widely in Europe and America, particularly in England (where he was at one time the Spanish Minister) and in the United States (where he married an American). During World War I he was a foreign correspondent for *La Prensa* of Buenos Aires.

As a novelist, his works form a bridge between the realism of the nineteenth century and the new trends of the twentieth. His masterpiece is, without doubt, *Belarmino and Apolonio* (1921). In it he treats symbolically the conflict between the life of the mind and life in reality. Among his best also is *Tigre Juan* (1926), which has been translated into English; it is a symbolic study of virility and the Don Juan theme. The locale of the novel (like many others) is "Pilares," a provincial city which is in fact Oviedo, Pérez de Ayala's birthplace, which was also mercilessly dissected by "Clarín." This city is as intimately connected with the work of Pérez de Ayala as Dublin is with James Joyce.

In addition to his work as a novelist, he has produced fine poetry which gives full play to his brilliant intellect and his seemingly limitless vocabulary. He is, moreover, a literary critic of considerable note.

Pérez de Ayala is also a distinguished writer of short stories. His two best collections are *Prometheus* (1916) and *The Heart of the World* (1924). From the latter comes the short story translated here. It will be noted that the action takes place in the University of "Pilares" (which is, of course, his alma mater, the University of Oviedo), and affords him an opportunity for some wry comments on the educational system in Spain.

The Substitute Professor

WHAT I AM about to relate happened some time ago, before Don Clemente came to live in Reicastro with his six daughters and his son-in-law. The events recounted here took place, as we shall see, in Pilares, the provincial capital in whose university Don Clemente had the fortune—or misfortune—to serve for a time as a substitute professor.

The six girls were in the dining room, which revealed extreme poverty: a pine table covered with a piece of oilcloth, ten wicker chairs, a weak electric light bulb without a shade, and that was all. The busy girls were bent over their tasks: some were embroidering, others were sewing or darning, still others were doing lace-work. They were sisters, the six of them, and each had the name of a virtue: Clemencia, Caridad, Socorro, Esperanza, Olvido and Piedad. They were poorly but neatly dressed, and carefully groomed.

Clemencia, the eldest, rose to her feet: "Didn't you hear that?"

Her five sisters stopped working, their needles poised in mid-air. Each cocked her head to one side, let her eyes stray from her work, and listened intently. They looked like five birds suddenly startled.

Clemencia, her arm outstretched, was pointing silently toward the door. Finally she affirmed quietly: "It's Papa."

Abandoning their work, they flew in a great gay

flock helter-skelter down the length of the hallway to the door at the head of the stairs. At that moment Don Clemente Iribarne was just coming in, holding his hat in his hand and wiping his brow, perspiring despite the winter weather. They all surrounded their father, struggling to be the first to hug him, and all asked at the same time: "What happened, Papa, what happened?"

"Let me catch my breath, you silly girls! Come into the dining room and I'll tell you."

He hung his hat on a nail in the hallway and went into the dining room, followed by his six daughters.

Don Clemente had one of those long, thin heads with glowing grey hair that appear again and again in paintings of Spanish men, whether portraying a nobleman or a rogue, a cardinal or a layman, a grandee or a beggar, an ascetic or a tippler, a mythological god or an apostle, a philosopher or a soldier; one of those heads we cannot quite identify, but remember having seen somewhere: in Velázquez' *The Coronation of Bacchus,* or as one of Zurbarán's monks, or a martyr by Ribera, or a water carrier by Murillo; in short, the classic Spanish stoic features. In Don Clemente's face could be seen nobility of character and austere intelligence. From the look of his frayed and shiny suit and mended shirt one could deduce the scarcity of his means and the dignity of his life.

The six daughters were attractive, but their charm was not due to wittiness or to a coquettish expression; nor did it come from their finely-chiselled features, but rose rather from the harmonious combination of modesty and serenity in their faces—a kind of visible manifestation of their inner spirit. They were like the images of those simple virgins—sweet rather than beautiful—that are seen in hermitages and village churches.

"At last, daughters," said Don Clemente, "I am a professor at the University."

The girls clapped their hands, and then with the tips of their fingers threw kisses at their father: "Tell us; tell us about it!"

"The meeting was quite a long one. Faculty politics were in evidence, but justice prevailed. Today I became a substitute professor in the new Faculty of Science, and tomorrow I shall give my first lecture in chemistry."

"What about Ayuso?" asked Clemencia.

"He has resigned his post on the ground that he is too busy. The truth is that he doesn't know chemistry. It was absurd . . . how was Ayuso going to teach advanced chemistry? He had become a professor through outside influence, but he knows absolutely nothing about chemistry."

"And the salary?" Clemencia asked.

"I don't know as yet . . . I suppose the stipend will be a thousand pesetas."

"A thousand pesetas!" the girls exclaimed, dazzled.

"It isn't much," Don Clemente added, "but it's still a thousand pesetas; and with my two thousand as an assistant teacher at the Institute, and what you, dear daughters, add with your labors, we shall have a decent —if modest—income. And now, enough of this talking; I have to study, and prepare for tomorrow's lecture."

He left the room and returned shortly with a volume on chemistry. The girls were working. The professor was studying.

It is a tradition in Spanish universities and institutes that students consider substitute professors as just a joke. When the regular professor is absent for a short time the substitute comes to replace him; but since there is only one substitute to cover all the Departments, whose subject matter varies widely, it is evident that the professor cannot be a true scholar in any of them. For this reason he lacks the authority of scientific learning, and in the majority of cases the regular professor does not hide his disdain for the substitute. This feeling is transmitted to the students. Thus it is that a substitute teaches only ten or twenty days a year, and not to cover the material that the regular professor has to omit from his lectures due to absence, but simply to comply with a regulation that prohibits interruptions during the course of the term.

It so happens that the substitute professor has no educational authority: his opinion and grades have no weight at the end of the semester, which is the time of woeful reckoning. The students know, therefore, that during the substitute's classes they can commit all kinds of misdeeds without fear of the consequences. When the custodian announces that the regular professor cannot come that day, and that the substitute will take over the class, the students smack their lips in anticipation of a wild spree.

All substitutes are the victims of jokes, wisecracks and nasty remarks—occasionally very cruel ones. But no substitute, in the long history of picaresque Spanish academic life, had to endure such extremely malicious pranks as Don Clemente Iribarne. Poor Don Clemente was so good-natured that even the boys in the third year at the Institute used to make outrageous fun of him right to his face. This ridicule contrasted with the love and adoration of his daughters, who were completely ignorant of what went on. Their father used to tell them a thousand white lies, and they believed that he was the most respected and beloved teacher at the Institute. They were proud of him.

The family lived in a small, dingy apartment house in a working class neighborhood. In their building, never reached by news of the academic world, the professor and his daughters enjoyed great prestige.

"What a country this is!" the women of the neighborhood used to say when they got together for a talk-fest. "A university professor—and in his house they are starving!"

They were not exactly starving, but they did eat very frugally indeed, and even this was due to the fact that the daughters took in work. The girls thought it demeaning for a professor's daughters to be employed at such lowly tasks, particularly in darning trousers and other types of men's clothing (Clemencia was skilful at this—she could darn better than any other girl in Pilares), so they resorted to a stratagem. It was this: other girls in the neighborhood would call for and deliver the work as if it were their own.

The daughters' own dresses were so cheap, and usually so threadbare, that they did not dare go out into the street during the day because they were ashamed to be seen in broad daylight, not so much for their own sake as out of respect for their father's social standing. Since the girls always lived indoors in virtuous seclusion, their faces—like their souls—were as white as communion wafers. Sundays they would go to mass at dawn, and weekdays they would go out after dark through unfrequented streets. Wearing veils that came down over their eyes, they would walk in twos, with Don Clemente beside the pair that brought up the rear. In order not to wear out their shoes they would walk lightly, scarcely stepping firmly on the soles of their feet. This gave them a certain graceful charm as they minced along in measured movements. Occasionally, just for a joke, some student would greet them by doffing his hat with an exaggerated sweep, and the girls, taking it seriously, would feel an emotion of contentment deep inside, coupled with tenderness toward their father.

Don Clemente had his eyes on his chemistry book, but his thoughts went wandering off into other channels. "If those boys at the Institute," he thought, "are so fresh with me, what won't those young men at the University be capable of doing? Logically, of course, they should be more sensible and respectful because they are older. Moreover, I am taking over the class completely and giving them their final examinations, and they will be careful of what they do—if not out of respect, then out of fear of failing the course." And with these and other distressing thoughts he spent his time and was unable to prepare for his lecture.

"When are we having supper?" he asked, raising his eyes from his book.

"Whenever you wish," Clemencia answered. And she added: "Have you finished your preparation?"

"Pshaw! I've studied a bit . . . but I've decided that the best thing to do tomorrow—and in keeping with tradition—will be to introduce myself to the students, say a few words, and then dismiss the class."

"How good you are!" his daughters said, deeply touched.

They all sat down to a cold supper of leftovers from lunch; and then, so as not to use electricity, they went to bed. But Don Clemente did not sleep.

The next day, on his way to the University, his legs were trembling. He went into the classroom, mounted the lecture platform, and remained standing there as the students filed in. The lecture room seats rose in ascending tiers, and they filled up immediately. Don Clemente looked up with frightened eyes at that swarming, noisy crowd, which seemed to be plunging down upon him. All the students were full-grown men. Some of them had been Don Clemente's pupils as boys at the Institute, but now they were sporting bristling mustaches. One had a full, black beard. Don Clemente was terrified.

"Gentlemen," he stammered, "as I accept the great honor of taking over this professorship and addressing you, what I want . . . most of all . . . is for you to look upon me not as a professor, but as a friend—better yet, a father."

At this, Pancho Benavides, a handsome, charming and wealthy young man who was the ringleader of all student disorders at the University, stood up and said: "That statement deeply stirs the most sensitive strings in our hearts. Hurrah for our father!"

"Hurrah!" the class responded.

"We applaud our father," Benavides said in conclusion. And there was a round of applause that lasted for five minutes.

Don Clemente had serious doubts about the sincerity of that manifestation, but in any event he placed his hand over his heart, bowed slightly in acknowledgement, and felt that he should say something. He continued talking, and after each sentence the prolonged applause was repeated. When his speech had ended, the students came down and flocked around the professor's desk.

"Now, in order to celebrate this occasion, you must treat us to something," said the bearded student, Acisclo

Zarracina, who had an appearance and a voice that were striking.

"How do you mean, treat you?" stammered Don Clemente, who never carried any money with him.

"Well, just treat us," asserted Zarracina, slamming his fist on the desk.

"Don't get excited, Zarracina," interrupted Alejandrín Serrín, a chubby, florid, mild-mannered young man.

"Treat us to cigarettes. You certainly must have some cigarettes on you," added Zarracina.

Don Clemente didn't dare answer. Yes, he had some cigarettes: his daughters bought him a pack every five days. That morning they had bought one. Several students began to feel the professor's pockets.

"Now, now, let me alone! Yes, I'll treat you to cigarettes. I take great pleasure in doing so—the occasion warrants it." And he handed over his pack to the students.

Under cover of the confusion produced by this, Pancho Benavides smeared the sweat-band of Don Clemente's hat with ink; then he dumped some powder into the hat and left it bottom up.

"All right, all right," sighed Don Clemente, pushing his way through the crowd of students. Mechanically, he picked up his hat and put it on his head. A shower of greenish powder came down over his eyes. He removed his hat and revealed his forehead, all inky. The students ran outside, laughing uproariously.

Don Clemente reached home.

"How was it?" his daughters asked him anxiously.

"Don't you know? It turns out that I am a fine lecturer."

And Don Clemente told them—in his own way—

about the success of his first class as a professor at the University. His daughters listened, enraptured.

After supper Clemencia asked her father, "Aren't you going to smoke?"

"Not now, daughter; I had forgotten all about it because I'm so busy with my lecture. . . ."

"My goodness, Papa!"

And a little later: "But aren't you going to smoke?"

"Yes, yes . . . Hush . . . Now where is my pack of cigarettes? No doubt I left it in the Faculty Room. Well, no matter. I'll read over tomorrow's lesson." And he began to study how to obtain hydrogen.

The next day he went to the University early so as to set up beforehand the apparatus needed to obtain hydrogen. The class began, and Don Clemente started his demonstration. Bent over the jars and tubes, he kept manipulating them industriously. He was wearing a slate-colored lab coat made of a heavy fabric woven in Palma de Mallorca. It had cost him five dollars. The students were gathered around him, watching his demonstration.

Pancho Benavides placed a small piece of lighted wood on Don Clemente's back, and the lab coat began to scorch.

"I seem to smell something burning," remarked Don Clemente.

The students said they smelled nothing. Soon the burning went through the lab coat to his jacket, his vest, his shirt, and finally reached his skin; at this point Don Clemente straightened up with a jump and gave a cry of pain. With a wet handkerchief Alejandrín Serrín snuffed out the sparks. Don Clemente uttered no word of complaint.

"That will be all for today, if you please," he said with trembling lips and eyes brimming with bitterness.

When he reached home he exclaimed, "My dear daughters! A great misfortune has occurred." And he showed them the holes burned through the back of his clothing, explaining that there had been an accident in the laboratory during the demonstration. "But," he continued, "the worst thing is this: How can I go out of the house now? This is the only suit I own—and where can I get the money for another? What a misfortune!"

"Don't worry, Papa," said Clemencia, the girl who could work miracles with her darning, as she examined the damage closely. "I've rewoven more difficult spots so that nobody could notice them."

And so it was. Don Clemente's clothing looked like new the next day in class, to the great astonishment of the students. Irritated by this seeming invulnerability of the professor, they determined to employ more energetic procedures.

Day by day the scandalous abuse by the class kept increasing. The greater the tolerance and forbearance shown by the professor, the more uncontrollable the students became. But the unruliness of the class reached such extremes that Don Clemente realized he ought to stand his ground somehow, or else resign his professorship. The expedient he hit upon was this: the laboratory's fire extinguisher had a kind of hose attachment with a spraying nozzle; he filled it with ink and put it on his desk, near at hand, before the class began.

It was a sunny spring day. No sooner had the students entered when Pancho Benavides took the floor:

"Professor, you have probably noticed the contrast between the bright beauty of the day and the grimy gloom of these halls and classrooms. Therefore, we have decided that there will be no lecture today, and we are going to spend this hour enjoying the sunshine. But because we are well brought-up young men we have come to inform you. So then, good-bye."

Don Clemente, who had placed his hand upon the extinguisher, looked at the fine, elegant clothes worn by Benavides and thought what a pity it would be to ruin them. He confined himself to replying:

"Mr. Benavides, I can take no account of your words. I am the professor here, and no one gives orders except me. Let us begin the lecture."

Zarracina stood up, and turning toward the class he clenched his fists and cried: "Caramba! We do what we want here! Outside!"

"No one goes outside!" exclaimed Don Clemente. And losing his head, he pointed the nozzle toward the terrible Zarracina and sprayed him with ink from head to foot.

Zarracina stood there stupefied for a moment. He quickly recovered himself and advanced furiously toward the professor's desk; but a new blast of ink in the face stopped him in his tracks. The class took Zarracina's part, and rained down an assortment of objects aimed at the professor's head. There were several rushes, but the torrents of ink always beat back the attacking groups.

The conflict was continuing amid a great uproar when the door of the room opened and the President of the University appeared. Suddenly hostilities ceased.

"What is this?" asked the President, looking at Don Clemente with cold severity.

Don Clemente, pale, tottering, and with his head hung low, mumbled a few words of explanation.

"Just what is your idea of the dignity of the professorship?" asked the President harshly, staring at Don Clemente with a look of contempt and revulsion. And he continued:

"We shall have a meeting of the Faculty, and we shall see what is to be done about you."

The President was on the point of leaving when the chubby Alejandrín Serrín stepped forward to the center of the class and stated calmly and firmly:

"Mr. President, the fault was ours—all ours—today and every day. Let us just see if there is one member of the class who will dare to contradict me. Is the fault ours, or not?" he cried, facing his classmates.

Several unidentified voices answered: "It is ours."

The President left in a bad humor.

When Don Clemente reached home his startled daughters asked him:

"What is the matter? You look as though you've been weeping."

"Yes, I have been weeping—and I am still weeping," he answered, wiping his eyes. And he told them that through intrigues on the part of other professors the President had come into his classroom and had begun to upbraid him, but that the President had had to stop and correct himself because the students—as one man—had declared themselves wholeheartedly in favor of Don Clemente. And he concluded by saying, "This is deeply touching!"

"Yes, indeed," said his daughters, much moved.

There was no faculty meeting to deliberate about Don Clemente. After the day of the great scandal the students agreed, in a friendly interview with the professor, that the best way to avoid new and regrettable incidents would be for no one to attend class who did not wish to. From then on, only a half dozen students came to class; on some days, however, when they had nothing better to do, a fair-sized group of students would drop in and renew the disturbances as before. Invariably, the ringleader and spearhead was Pancho Benavides.

The end of the term came around. On the day of the final examination in chemistry, Pancho Benavides rose early, bought a box of Havana cigars, and started off for Don Clemente's house. He had memorized exactly what he was going to say: "My dear Don Clemente, I do not know a word of chemistry, but I need a passing grade. This is a box of cigars; this is a pistol. If you pass me, I shall present you with the box of cigars; if you fail me, I shall shoot you. The choice is up to you."

Pancho knocked at the door, and the professor himself came to open it. Don Clemente was really fond of Pancho in spite of his deviltry, but when he saw him at the house he was filled with anxiety because the student might be disrespectful to him in front of his daughters.

"What is it, Mr. Benavides? Wait a moment; I'll come with you and we can talk on the way to school . . . I was just getting ready to leave."

"No, sir. I must speak to you inside your house."

"But I was really just getting ready to leave."

"Would you throw me out of your house?"

Don Clemente did not know what to do or to say. The girls were peering out of the dining room door. Clemencia came down the hallway to where her father was and said:

"Why don't you ask this gentleman to come in, Papa?"

"Yes, yes, of course . . . gladly," Don Clemente murmured, panic-stricken. "He is one of my students. This is one of my daughters."

Benavides and Clemencia acknowledged the introduction, and Benavides came inside the house. The
hallway was dark, and the young man groped for
the hatrack.

"What are you looking for?" asked Don Clemente.

"The hatrack," Benavides answered.

"We don't have one," Clemencia remarked laugh-
ingly. "You see? No one can judge better than one of
Papa's students how unjust the Government is to hold
back—and at a low salary—the most distinguished
professor in the University, the one most loved by his
students."

At this moment they were entering the dining room.
As Benavides listened to Clemencia he felt a kind of
chill or tremor that ran up and down his back and
settled in the nape of his neck and his eyelids.

"What salary do you make, Don Clemente, if I
am not being indiscreet?"

"Before the chemistry lectureship, two thousand
pesetas; now, three thousand. After deductions, about
twenty-five hundred."

"And these young ladies—they are your daughters?"

"All of them, Mr. Benavides. They are angels,"
Don Clemente murmured, almost breathlessly.

"Oh, Papa!" the six virtues exclaimed with respectful
modesty, lowering their heads like six white lilies.

As if entranced, the girls gazed at that young man
who looked so elegant—a pupil of their father's, and

therefore subordinate to him, of course. Benavides was
looking at them discreetly; his gaze rested longest upon
Clemencia's face.

"I should like to speak to you privately, Don
Clemente—in your study, for example," Benavides
asked him.

"This is my study, my dear Benavides."

"I thought I heard them say it was the dining room. . . ."

"Of course. It serves for everything."

"And your books?"

"Ah, they are in a drawer in my room!"

"Then I shall tell you here what I have to say. I am bringing you a small present: a box of Havana cigars. No, please don't refuse them. It is just a token of my esteem. I do not expect you to pass me; I am not prepared for the examination, and so to save you the distress of failing me I have decided not to sit for the examination until September. This is what I came to tell you. On the other hand, you have been so kind to me during the semester that I felt I should express my gratitude in some way."

Clemencia's eyes, and those of the other virtues, shone through their tears. Don Clemente lowered his head. Benavides felt a lump in his throat, and in his heart there was a mixture of tenderness, remorse, and defiance.

Pancho Benavides and Clemencia Iribarne were married two years later. Now Don Clemente teaches at the Magdalene Fathers Junior College, where he is Adjunct Professor of Psychology, Civil Law, Algebra, Intermediate French, and Applied Art—of all of which he knows exactly nothing. Pancho and Clemencia, with three children now, are as happy as young people in romantic novels. And Don Clemente attends the meetings of the learned Scorpion Society, where they consider him a prodigy of wisdom because he never opens his mouth.

Pío Baroja (1872–1956)

. . . came from the rugged Basque country in northern Spain, close to the French frontier. Baroja studied medicine, and earned his doctor's degree; after a year as a physician in the Basque region he abandoned that career and moved to Madrid. With his brother he managed a bakery business; at the same time he began to write, and produced two fine volumes of short stories about life in the Basque country: *Sombre Lives* (1900) and *Basque Idylls* (1901). From the latter comes the story translated here. It is a universal favorite on both sides of the Atlantic: many Basques have emigrated to Spanish America, and for them it is a nostalgic touch of the homeland.

When his first novel (*Road to Perfection*) was published in 1902, he decided to devote himself entirely to writing, and has since become Spain's most forceful and prolific novelist of this century. Baroja's works deal with many regions of Spain, and with other countries as well; his best have his *patria chica*—the Basque country—as the background.

He was a rebel and an ultra-individualist, and could conform to no political party. He was against practically every facet of organized society, but passionately sincere in his criticism of the world in general and of Spain in particular. For the ills of mankind, Doctor Baroja saw no remedy: all suggested cures would be worse than the disease.

The two pervading elements in his novels are utter pessimism, and its antidote, dynamic action: Schopenhauer and Nietzsche were his favorite philosophers. Typical works that illustrate these feelings are *The Tree of Science* (1911), based on his own youthful struggles; *Paradox, the King* (1906), a corrosive socio-political satire; and the semi-historical series of novels called the *Memoirs of a Man of Action* (1913–1935).

Baroja writes in a rapid, nervous, kaleidoscopic—sometimes careless—style. Often there seems to be no formal plot, just a series of events that make no sense—like life itself. The one common element in all his books is a high sense of adventure. His best heroes are wanderers, men who see through the illusions of life so clearly that they exert no effort to struggle against its sterile stupidity. This is the apathy—the *abulia*—that preoccupied the intellectuals of the Generation of 1898. Elizabide, the central figure in the following short story, is a typical Baroja character.

Elizabide the Rover

> *¿Cer zala usté cenuben*
> *enamoratzia?*
> *¿Sillan ishiri eta*
> *guitarra jotzia?* [1]

FREQUENTLY, while he was working in that old garden, Elizabide the Rover would say to himself when he saw Maintoni pass by, on her way back from church, "What can she be thinking? Is she satisfied with her life?"

Maintoni's life seemed so strange to him! It was natural that someone like him, who had always knocked about the world from pillar to post, should delight in the calm and quiet of the village; but mustn't she, who had never left that locality, feel some desire to go to the theater, to parties and other amusements, or to enjoy a different life that was more colorful and active? And since Elizabide the Rover could find no answer to his question, he kept on turning the earth with his hoe philosophically.

"She is a strong woman," he thought later. "Her

---

[1] Pío Baroja often interpolates Basque words and phrases in his stories to lend local color; unless they are well-known (words like *jai-alai*, for example) he translates them into Castilian for his readers in the rest of Spain and in Spanish America. These lines are from an old Basque folk song which means: 'Just what did you think falling in love was? Sitting on a chair and playing the guitar?'

spirit is so serene, so sunny, that it makes you wonder . . . Just scientific curiosity—purely scientific, of course."

And Elizabide the Rover, satisfied with his self-assurance that he was not personally involved in that curiosity, kept on working in the old garden next to his house.

He was a strange kind of fellow, this Elizabide the Rover. He combined all the good qualities—and the defects—of the coastal Basque: he was daring, cynical, lazy, and jovial. Lightheartedness and forgetfulness were his fundamental characteristics: nothing mattered to him, and he forgot everything. He had spent almost the entire amount of his slender capital during his wanderings through South America, as a newspaperman in one city, a businessman in another, selling cattle here and dealing in wines there. Many times he was on the verge of making his fortune, but through apathy he never succeeded. He was one of those men who just let themselves be carried along by events without ever protesting. He used to compare his life to one of those logs that go floating down the river and finally— if no one picks them up—drift out to sea.

His inertia and laziness were more mental than physical: it was his spirit that ran away with him many times. All he needed was to look at flowing water, or to gaze at a cloud or a star, and he would forget the most important project in his life; and if he didn't forget it because of this, he would abandon it for some other reason, often without knowing why.

Recently he had been on a ranch in Uruguay. As Elizabide had a pleasant personality and was not unattractive in appearance although he was already thirty-eight years old, the owner of the ranch offered him the hand of his daughter, who was quite a homely girl and in love with a mulatto. Elizabide rather liked the rough life on the ranch, so he agreed. The time for the wedding was near at hand, when he felt nostalgic for his home town, for the odor of new-mown hay in the highlands, and for the misty landscape of the Basque country. Since he never liked to make blunt explanations, one morning at dawn he told his fiancée's parents that he was going in to Montevideo to buy the wedding gift. He rode off on horseback, and then took the train; when he reached the capital he boarded a transatlantic liner, and after waving a fond farewell to South America he returned to Spain.

He reached his home town, a little village in the province of Guipúzcoa. He embraced his brother Ignacio, who was the pharmacist there, went to see his old nurse—whom he promised never to run away again—and settled down in his house. When the rumor spread around town that not only had he failed to make anything in South America but had actually lost money, everyone remembered that before leaving he already had the reputation of being a foolish, good-for-nothing rover.

He wasn't worried in the slightest about all this; he dug in his garden, and in his spare time worked at building a canoe to paddle on the river, which made the whole town angry.

Elizabide the Rover thought that his brother Ignacio, and the latter's wife and children, looked down upon him, and therefore he went to visit them only occasionally; but he soon saw that his brother and his sister-in-law thought well of him and reproached him because he did not come to see them. Elizabide began to visit his brother's house more frequently.

The pharmacist's home stood by itself on the edge of town. On the side that faced the road it had a garden surrounded by a wall, and over it hung branches of dark green laurel that partially shielded the front of the house from the north wind. Just beyond the garden was the pharmacy.

The house had no balconies—just windows, and these seemed to have been placed in the wall without any symmetrical arrangement; this was due to the fact that some of them were bricked up.

When travelling by train or car through the northern provinces, haven't you seen isolated homes that made you envious, without knowing why? They seem to give the feeling that life must be good inside there, and one envisions a sweet and peaceful existence; the curtained windows hint at almost monastic interiors whose huge rooms are furnished with walnut chests and dressers, and enormous wooden beds; they suggest a calm and restful way of life in which the hours pass slowly, measured by the old grandfather clock that tick-tocks loudly in the night. . . .

The pharmacists's home was one like that. In the garden there were hyacinths, heliotropes, rosebushes and huge hydrangeas that grew as high as the balconies on the lower floor. Spilling down from the top of the garden wall there came a cascade of single white roses that are called in Basque *choruas* (crazy) because they grow wild and break so easily, and because they wither and fall apart so soon.

When Elizabide the Rover—more confident now— went to his brother's home, the pharmacist and his wife, followed by all the children, showed him the house, spotless, sparkling and clean-smelling; then they went to see the garden, and here Elizabide saw

Maintoni for the first time. She was wearing a straw hat to protect her head, and was picking peas and putting them into her skirt. Elizabide and she greeted each other indifferently.

"We are going down to the river," the pharmacist's wife said to her sister. "Tell the girls to bring our chocolate there."

Maintoni went off toward the house, and the others, passing through a kind of long tunnel formed by pear trees whose branches spread out like the ribs of a fan, went down to a grove next to the river, where there was a rustic table and a stone bench. The sun, piercing the foliage, lighted up the bottom of the stream and revealed the round stones on the river bed; the fish, swimming around lazily, shone like silver. The air was wonderfully still beneath a serene and pure blue sky.

Before sunset the two girls came from the pharmacist's house carrying trays of chocolate and biscuits. The children fell upon the biscuits like little animals. Elizabide the Rover spoke of his travels, related some of his adventures, and had them all hanging upon his words. Maintoni was the only one who seemed not to be very enthusiastic about those tales.

"You'll come again tomorrow, Uncle Pablo, won't you?" the children asked him.

"Yes, I'll come."

And Elizabide the Rover went home. He thought of Maintoni, and dreamed about her. In his dream he saw her just as she was: small and slender, with dark, flashing eyes, and surrounded by her nieces and nephews, who were embracing and kissing her.

Since the eldest of the boys was in the third year of his secondary schooling, Elizabide devoted himself to giving the boy instruction in French, and Maintoni attended the lessons.

Elizabide was beginning to be concerned about his sister-in-law's sister, who was so steadfastly serene: he could not make out whether her soul was that of a child, with no desires or aspirations, or whether she was a woman who was indifferent to everything not directly related to the people living in her house. The Rover used to look at her in fascination and ask himself: "What can she be thinking?"

Once he felt bold and said to her, "Don't you ever think about getting married, Maintoni?"

"Me! Get married?"

"Why not?"

"Who is going to take care of the children if I get married? Besides, I'm already a *nescazarra* (an old maid)," she answered, laughing.

"An old maid at twenty-seven? Then I must be in the last stages of decrepitude—I'm thirty-eight!"

Maintoni said nothing in reply; she just smiled.

That night Elizabide was astonished to find that Maintoni was occupying his thoughts. "What kind of woman is she?" he said to himself. "She isn't haughty at all . . . or romantic either . . . but still in all. . . ."

At the river's edge, near a narrow defile, there was a spring that had a very deep pool; the water there seemed like glass, so still it was. Elizabide kept telling himself that perhaps Maintoni's soul was like that . . . but still in all . . . Her image did not fade, however; on the contrary, it kept growing larger.

Summer came. In the garden of the pharmacist's house the whole family would gather, along with Maintoni and Elizabide the Rover. Never was the latter more punctual than then—and never so happy and so miserable at the same time. At nightfall the sky was studded with stars, a pale light glowed in the heavens, and the toads all piped in chorus. Then the family conversation would become more intimate, and Maintoni, more relaxed, would talk more freely.

At nine o'clock, when they heard the bells on the stagecoach that went through town with its big lamp atop the driver's seat, the gathering would break up. Elizabide would walk home making plans for the next day; they always revolved about Maintoni.

Sometimes, when he was discouraged, he would ask himself: "Isn't it silly, after travelling all over the world, to come back to a little town and fall in love with a village girl?" And to think he wasn't bold enough to say anything to that woman who was so cool and composed!

The summer slipped by, and festival time arrived. The pharmacist and his family were getting ready to take part in the picnic and pilgrimage to Arnazabal as they did each year.

"You are coming along with us, aren't you?" the pharmacist asked his brother.

"Not I."

"Why not?"

"I don't feel like it."

"All right, all right. But I warn you that you'll be left alone, because even the maids are coming with us."

"Are you going, too?" said Elizabide to Maintoni.

"Yes, indeed; I should say so! I love picnics!"

"Don't listen to her; it's not that," the pharmacist said. "She's going to see the doctor over in Arnazabal, a young man who was very attentive to her last year."

"And why not?" exclaimed Maintoni, smiling.

Elizabide the Rover turned pale, then reddened; but he said nothing.

The night before the pilgrimage the pharmacist asked his brother again: "So then, are you going, or not?"

"All right; I'll go," the Rover mumbled.

The following day they all arose early and set out along the highway leading from the town. Later they took to trails, crossed meadows covered with tall grass and purple foxglove, and went into the woods. The morning was cool and damp, and the countryside was wet with dew; the sky was a very pale blue, with little puffs of cottony clouds that were shredding into thin strands. At ten in the morning they reached Arnazabal, a highland town with its church, its *jai-alai* court in the square, and two or three streets of stone houses.

They entered a country house that belonged to the pharmacist's wife, and went into the kitchen. Then came the exchange of greetings and the warm welcome by the old lady of the house, who left off her work of throwing wood on the fire and rocking a child's cradle. She rose from the low fireplace next to which she was seated, greeted them all, and kissed Maintoni, Maintoni's sister, and the children. She was a thin, withered old woman whose white hair was covered with a black kerchief; her long nose, set in a wrinkled face, hooked down over a toothless mouth.

"And you are the one who was in South America?" the old woman said, turning to Elizabide.

"Yes, I am the one who was there."

As ten o'clock had struck, and high mass was beginning at that hour, only the old woman stayed at home; all the others went to church.

Before dinner the pharmacist, with the aid of his

sister-in-law and the children, fired a whole flock of
rockets from the windows; then every one went down
to the dining room. There were more than twenty
people at the table, among them the town doctor,
who sat near Maintoni and directed to her and her
sister an endless series of gallantries and little attentions. Elizabide the Rover felt such deep sadness then
that he thought of leaving town and returning to
South America. During dinner Maintoni looked frequently at Elizabide.

"That is to make fun of me," he thought. "She has
guessed that I love her and is flirting with the other
man. It looks as though I'll be off to the Gulf of
Mexico again."

When dinner ended it was after four o'clock, and
the dancing had begun. The doctor, never leaving
Maintoni's side, kept on devoting his attention to her,
and she kept looking at Elizabide.

At nightfall, when the festivities were at their height,
the *aurrescu* began. The young men, hands joined,
kept circling the plaza preceded by drummers; two of
the young men left the line, conferred, hesitated, and
then, removing their berets, invited Maintoni to be the
leader, the queen of the dance. Speaking in Basque, she
tried to dissuade them, and looked at her brother-in-law,
who was smiling, at her sister, who was also smiling,
and at Elizabide, who was plunged in gloom.

"Go ahead; don't be foolish," her sister said.

And the dance began, with all its ceremony and
ritual that recalled an earlier, heroic age. When the
aurrescu was over the pharmacist asked his wife to
dance the fandango with him, and the doctor asked
Maintoni.

Darkness fell. Bonfires were lighted in the plaza,
and people began to think about the return trip. After

drinking chocolate at the summer house, the pharmacist's family and Maintoni set out along the road home.
Off in the distant woods, pilgrims returning from the
picnic could be heard shouting *irrintzis,* their wild,
Basque cries. In the thickets the fireflies glowed like
bluish stars, and the toads could be heard piping their
clear notes in the crystal silence of the peaceful night.

From time to time as they were going down a hill, the
pharmacist thought it a good idea for everyone to hold
hands, and they would go down the slope singing:

> *Aita San Antoniyo Urquiyolacua,*
> *Ascoren biyotzeco santo devotua.* [2]

In spite of the fact that Elizabide wanted to keep
away from Maintoni because he was angry with her,
it happened that she found herself next to him.
When the chain was formed, she would give him her
hand, small, soft and warm. Suddenly the pharmacist,
who was first in line, would decide to stop and to push
back; then they would all bump into each other, and
sometimes Maintoni would tumble into Elizabide's arms.
She would scold her brother-in-law, and would look at
the Rover, who was still dejected.

"What are you so sad about?" Maintoni asked him in
a teasing voice, and her dark eyes shone in the night.

"I don't know, really. Just the wicked perverseness
of a man who—without reason—is saddened by the
joys of others."

"But you're not wicked," said Maintoni. And she
looked at him so searchingly with her dark eyes that
Elizabide the Rover thought the very stars would
notice how stirred he was.

[2] Baroja translates this into Castilian for his readers, with the
following meaning: "Father St. Anthony of Urquiola is the saint to
whom many hearts are devoted."

"No, I am not wicked," he murmured. "But I am a foolish good-for-nothing, just as the whole town says."

"And is that what worries you—what is said by people who don't know you?"

"Yes. I'm afraid it may be the truth. And for a man who has to leave for South America again, that is a depressing fear."

"Leave! Are you going to leave?" Maintoni murmured sadly.

"Yes."

"But why?"

"Oh, I can't tell you why."

"And if I should guess?"

"Then I would be very sorry; you would make fun of me, because I'm old. . . ."

"Not at all!"

"And I'm poor."

"It makes no difference."

"Oh, Maintoni! Really? You wouldn't refuse me?"

"No. Just the opposite."

"Then . . . you will love me as I love you?"

"Always, always. . . ."

Maintoni rested her head upon Elizabide's chest, and he kissed her chestnut hair.

"Maintoni! Over here!" her sister called. She drew away from him, but he kept looking at her again and again. And they all continued walking toward the town along the deserted roads.

All about him the night vibrated mysteriously, and the stars in the sky seemed to throb. And Elizabide the Rover, his heart flooded with unutterable delights and smothered in happiness, kept looking with wide eyes at a star that was far away—very far away—and he talked to it in a soft voice. . . .

Miguel de Unamuno (1864–1936)

. . . was the dean of the Generation of 1898. A Basque—and an arch-individualist like Baroja—he was educated in Bilbao and at the University of Madrid. He returned to his native region and taught there while studying to take the examinations for a university professorship. He won the chair of Classical Languages at the University of Salamanca in 1891, and ten years later was appointed Rector of the University. Unlike Baroja, who never married, Unamuno wed his childhood sweetheart. They had nine children.

He was frequently in trouble with the authorities for his opposition to the monarchy and to the dictatorship of Primo de Rivera. He went into voluntary exile in France from 1924 to 1930. But when the Republic came into power in 1931 he mistrusted it, despite the honors it accorded him; and later, when the Spanish Civil War broke out in 1936, he finally denounced both sides.

Unamuno was essentially a philosopher. His all-abiding preoccupation was the struggle to reconcile Reason and Faith, the world of the spirit and the world of reality which includes death. He came to the conclusion that the individual soul is the only reality. His greatest work, a collection of philosophical essays, deals with this theme; its title is *The Tragic Sense of Life in Men and Peoples* (1912). And his work *The Christ of Velázquez* (1920), a series of lyrical and intellectual meditations, expresses much the same idea in poetic form; it is rated as the finest religious poetry since the days of the great Spanish mystics of the sixteenth century.

Unamuno also cultivated the novel, the drama, the novelette and the short story. All reveal the same agonizing preoccupation with the profound moral issues of life, death, and immortality. The story here translated is typical of Unamuno's philosophy of life as a constant struggle. It is taken from his collection of short stories titled, significantly, *The Mirror of Death* (1913).

In addition to his great work as a writer, Unamuno was also an outstanding teacher. In the early 1930's he was the Grand Old Man at the *Residencia de Estudiantes* in Madrid, that remarkable educational institution which brought together such men as Ortega y Gassett, Juan Ramón Jiménez and García Lorca, who studied, wrote, taught and exchanged views there. After the siesta hour Unamuno would sit in the garden beneath a tree and talk with his students about any topic that came to his mind, while his fingers were busy with a pair of scissors and a piece of paper. When the bell rang for classes to resume, he would end his discussion—and open up the paper with a string of cut-outs: camels, clowns, or other simple figures! To have studied with him was indeed a rare intellectual experience.

Juan Manso: A Dead Men's Tale

AND NOW for a story.

While he was on this wicked earth Juan Manso was a simple soul, a harmless fellow who during his whole life had never hurt a fly. As a child, when he played donkey with his friends, he was always the donkey. Later, his comrades confided in him about their love affairs, and when he grew to full manhood his acquaintances still used to greet him with an affectionate "Hello, little Johnny!"

His favorite maxim was from the Chinese: "Never commit yourself, and stick to the person who can help you the most."

He loathed politics, hated business, and avoided everything that might upset the even tenor of his ways.

He lived on a small income which he spent in its entirety without ever touching the capital. He was quite devout, would never contradict anyone, and as he had a bad opinion of everybody he spoke well of them.

If you mentioned politics to him he would say: "I'm nothing—neither one side nor the other: I don't care which party runs the government. I'm just a poor sinner who wants to live at peace with everyone."

His meekness, however, was of no avail against the finality of death. It was the only definite thing he ever did in his life.

An angel armed with a great flaming sword was sorting out souls according to the sign made upon them as they went by an enrollment desk which they had to pass as they departed from this world and went through a kind of immigration control where angels and devils were sitting side by side in friendly fashion examining documents to see if they were all in order.

The entrance to the registration room looked like the scene outside the box office on the day of a big bullfight. There were so many people milling around, pushing and shoving, with everyone in such a hurry to learn his fate, and such was the hubbub raised by the curses, entreaties, insults and excuses in the thousands of languages, dialects and jargons of this world, that Juan Manso said to himself:

"Who says I have to get mixed up in all this? There must be some very rough characters around here."

He said this *sotto voce,* so no one could hear him. The fact is that the angel with the great flaming sword paid not the slightest attention to him, so he was able to slip past and start on his way to Heaven.

He walked along very quietly all by himself. From time to time happy groups would pass by, chanting litanies; some were dancing wildly, which seemed to him not quite a proper thing for the blessed to be doing on their way up to Heaven. When he reached the heights he found a long line of people standing beside the walls of Paradise, and a few angels keeping order like policemen on earth. Juan Manso got on the very end of the line.

Shortly a humble Franciscan friar came along, and he was so clever in advancing pathetic arguments as to why he was in such a hurry to get inside right away that Juan Manso gave him his place in line, saying to himself:

"It's a good idea to make friends for yourself even in Heaven."

The next man to come along, though not a Franciscan, wanted the same privilege, and the same thing happened. In short, there wasn't a pious soul who did not trick Juan Manso out of his place; his reputation for meekness ran along the whole line, and was handed down as a continuing tradition among the constantly-changing crowd there. And Juan Manso stayed where he was, the prisoner of his own good reputation.

Centuries went by—or so it seemed to Juan Manso, for it took that much time for the meek little lamb to begin to lose his patience. Finally one day he happened to meet a wise and saintly bishop who turned out to be the great-great-grandson of one of Manso's brothers. Juan voiced his complaints to his great-great-grandnephew, and the wise and saintly bishop offered to intercede for him when he came before the Eternal Father. On the strength of this, Juan yielded his place to the wise and saintly bishop who, when he entered Heaven, quite properly went straight to the Eternal Father to pay Him his respects. He concluded his little talk with The Almighty, who listened absent-mindedly and said:

"Wasn't there something else you wanted to say?"

And with His glance He searched the depths of the bishop's heart.

"Lord, permit me to intercede for one of Thy servants who 'is out there at the very tip end of the line. . . ."

"Don't beat about the bush," thundered The Lord. "You mean Juan Manso."

"Yes, Lord, he is the one; Juan Manso, who. . . ."

"All right! All right! Let him look out for himself, and don't you get mixed up again in other people's affairs!" And turning to the angel who was introducing souls, He added: "Let the next one in!"

If anything is capable of marring the eternal happiness of a soul in everlasting bliss, we could say that the soul of the wise and saintly bishop was troubled. But at least, moved by pity, he went to Heaven's walls, next to which the long line was standing. He climbed up, and calling to Juan Manso he said:

"Great-great-uncle, how sad I am about this—how very sad, my dear man! The Lord told me that you should look out for yourself, and that I shouldn't get mixed up in other people's affairs again. But . . . are you still at the end of the line? Come now, my dear man! Summon up some courage and don't yield your place again."

"Now he tells me!" exclaimed Juan Manso, shedding tears as big as chick-peas. But it was too late, for the tragic tradition was now attached to him: people no longer even asked him for his place, they just took it.

Crestfallen, he abandoned the line and began to wander about the lonely wastelands beyond the grave until he came upon many people, all downcast, walking along a road. He followed their footsteps and found himself at the gates of Purgatory.

"It will be easier to get in here," he said to himself, "and once inside they will send me directly to Heaven after I have been purified."

"Hey! Where are you going, my friend?"

Juan Manso turned around and found himself face to face with an angel who was wearing an academic mortarboard and had a pen behind his ear. He looked at Juan over the top of his glasses, had him turn around, and after examining him from head to foot frowned and said:

"H-m-m! *Malorum causa*—the root of all ills! You are completely grey, and I'm afraid to put you through our procedures for fear you'll melt. You would do better to go to Limbo."

"To Limbo!"

Upon hearing this, Juan Manso became indignant for the first time, for no man is so patient and long-suffering that he will stand for having an angel treat him like a complete idiot.

In desperation, he set out for Hell. Here there was no waiting line, nor anything like one. It had a broad entrance, from which came puffs of thick smoke and an infernal din. At the door a poor devil was playing a hand-organ and shrieking at the top of his voice:

"Come inside, gentlemen, step inside . . . Here you will see the human comedy . . . Anyone may enter. . . ."

Juan Manso closed his eyes.

"Hey, young man! Stop!" the poor devil said to him.

"Didn't you say that anyone might enter?"

"Yes, but . . . Look," said the poor devil earnestly, as he stroked his tail, "we still have some slight spark of conscience . . . and, after all . . . you?"

"All right, all right!" said Juan Manso, turning away because he could not stand the smoke.

And he heard the devil mutter to himself, "Poor fellow!"

"Poor fellow? Even the devil pities me!"

Desperate now to the point of madness, he began to bob around like a cork in mid-ocean as he crossed the vast spaces beyond the grave. From time to time he would meet other legendary lost souls.

One day, attracted by the appetizing odor that was coming from Heaven, he approached its walls to see what they were cooking inside. It was about time for sunset, and he saw that The Lord was coming out to enjoy the cool air in the gardens of Paradise. Juan Manso waited for Him near the wall, and when he saw His noble head he opened his arms wide in supplication and said in a rather indignant tone:

"Lord, Lord, didst Thou not promise the Kingdom of Heaven to the meek?"

"Yes, but to the enterprising, not to the weak-kneed."

And He turned His back on Juan.

An old legend recounts that The Lord, taking pity on Juan Manso, let him return to this wicked world, and that when he got here again he began to push people around right and left. When he died a second time, he shoved his way right past the famous line and slipped boldly into Paradise.

Now inside, he keeps repeating:

"Man has to fight his way through life on earth!"

Azorín (1873–   )

. . . is the pseudonym of José Martínez Ruiz, who adopted this name from the hero of two of his early novels, Antonio Azorín. He was born in the province of Alicante on the Mediterranean coast, a region that has produced few famous contemporary writers as compared, for example, with the Biscayan coast, which has produced a disproportionately large number of outstanding literary figures in modern times. He studied law, but abandoned his legal career in favor of letters. He did not, however, shut himself up in an ivory tower: he was elected to the Spanish parliament five times, and served twice in the cabinet as Assistant Secretary of Education.

It was Azorín, one of Spain's greatest literary critics, who coined the now-famous name, "Generation of 1898." Like most members of that introspective generation, he felt the strong pull of the heartland of Spain, Castile. His descriptions of it, particularly his evocations of its nostalgic past, are some of the most moving passages in modern Spanish prose. A feeling of melancholy pervades most of his writing. Unlike his good friend Pío Baroja, whose rapidly-written works abound in ebullient action, Azorín was a careful craftsman, and description, rather than narration, is his forte; the plot—if any—is entirely secondary, as in life itself. He was a conscious stylist, passionately in love with words, and his lyric, luminous prose abounds in words that evoke impressions of the slow passage of time—"the tragedy of time," as he calls it.

Azorín was also a fine dramatist: two of his best works in this field are *Old Spain* (1926), whose title is in English, and *Brandy, mucho Brandy* (1927). But it is as an essayist that he excels, particularly when he is describing the Castilian landscape or old Castilian towns.

As a prose stylist, he ranks second only to Valle-Inclán in contemporary Spanish literature; some critics feel that he ranks first. With deep sensitivity and a wealth of detail, Azorín interprets the spirit of Spain in his finest collections of essays: *The Castilian Soul* (1900), *Villages* (1905), and *Castile* (1912). In all of these we find an abiding sense of eternity: the past merges with the present, and all of time is one.

Azorín also wrote several volumes of delightful short stories. From the collection called *White on Blue* (1929) comes the tale selected for translation here. The central figure, Felix Vargas, is Martínez Ruiz himself in his later years (one of his introspective novels, published in 1928, is *Felix Vargas*), just as "Azorín" is the author as a young man. The nostalgic sense of the passage of time, as well as the sensitivity of his style, are clearly evident in this wistful tale.

The Children at the Beach

A STORY about children at the beach? All right. Let us begin.

Once upon a time there was a poet; his name was Felix Vargas. The poet is staying at the seaside in a sunny, spotless, spacious house. He is not a poor poet; he is, indeed, an exception among poets. And he has good taste. There was really no need to mention this, since he was a true poet.

The house has a terrace paved with huge flagstones. The poet loves stone: pebbly stone, the kind from Guadarrama; sandstone, soft and easy to work, but resistant when the winds lash it and the rains drench it; stone carved by an artisan's chisel into simple figures; rough, irregular stone that is set into walls with mortar.

The poet loves stone, and the sea. From the terrace of his summer home he has a splendid, sweeping view of the sea. By day the sea is blue, green, turquoise, grey, silver. At night the beam from a lighthouse up the coast flashes on and off, and the waves plash in regular rhythm with a soothing sound, a sound that delights the poet during those delicious, voluptuous

moments between dreaming and waking, just as he is
dropping off to sleep./

And here, on the beach, a few steps from the terrace,
among the bathers stretched out on the golden sand,
there are children, many children, an infinite number
of children, who come and go all morning long, romp-
ing and chattering. They run before the waves when
the waves advance; then they chase them and stamp
upon them and splash them with little bare feet when
the waves, after having exerted themselves by advancing toward the bathers, tire and retreat, only to attack
again at once./

The poet works in the early morning, when the
air is thin and cool, when the light is crystal-clear and
virgin-fresh. Then, toward noon, three or four or half a
dozen friends come to visit him. At this hour Felix
Vargas is a little tired of composing. The ladies and
gentlemen talk; but he listens dreamily, absently, to
their gay, gossipy chatter as if he were far away, as if a
curtain of mist had been lowered between him and
his friends. And only when Plácida Valle speaks does
it seem that the curtain is pierced and the poet hears
the words clearly and sharply.

Plácida Valle is tall and svelte, with a pleasingly
full but not overdeveloped bosom. The lines of her
shapely figure are softly curved, and her luscious lips
form a fresh red stroke across her expressive, mobile
face, now gay, now grave. Where does Plácida Valle
live? Up there, on the hill, in another charming
little house facing the sea. Solitude is not wholly
unpleasing to this woman; the years have been slipping
by, and life's pleasures, for Plácida, must be deep and
calm and stable. Plácida's whole being radiates
serenity and poise. When she speaks her words are

deliberate and discreet; her hand, a white, plump hand, moves with dignity and grace./Plácida never really says anything; she does not express opinions that are clever or profound; but the ordinary, everyday words she uses, pronounced in such a slow and solemn way, hold the poet like the sound of some rare, enchanting melody./

Plácida Valle speaks, and the poet, stretched out upon the chaise longue, raises himself slightly, looks at her, and listens in silence, enraptured. Can there be anything new in life for the poet? Fame has given him its pleasures; he appeals to the élite and to the public alike. To be an artist only for the few is to live confined in a narrow, limited, restricted milieu; one has the fervent approbation of some few disciples, of a handful of admirers. But what about that long, curious, eager look of a passerby who recognizes you? And that pleasant smile in a train, restaurant, or museum from some lady among your readers, who is following your works step by step? And that pleasing, special—and rewarding—response that your works produce in the populace at large? In the populace who, fortunately, through your work and similar works by your colleagues, are refining their taste little by little, striving to reach a lofty level of world peace and brotherhood. Felix Vargas the poet likes things that are select, exclusive, and intimate; but at the same time he would suffer a little if the general public were not acquainted with his work because it was directed toward a single group. He has, in the depths of his soul, in his innermost being, a mild disdain for the general public; but vanity perhaps, and perhaps sublime pity—pity for every human being—enter their protest and drag him gently but firmly from the narrow circle of the élite out into the broad world where the sun is bright and the winds blow.

Felix Vargas has seen everything, and he is a little weary of life. The clouds are low and grey this summer morning; the frolicking children on the golden sand keep coming and going. On the poet's terrace the callers have all chatted a while, and then have drifted off. No, not all. The stately Plácida Valle remains behind, as if her fancy has been caught in a little net of dreams, wishes and hopes. Plácida is turning the pages of a book without seeing the words, and Felix sends a puff of smoke up into the air.

These past few days a young critic has been calling upon him to ask him some details about his life. This returning from the present to the past is a torment for the poet. He is superstitious about time: it depresses him to recall the past; it might be said that the remembrance of things past, his past—his childhood, adolescence and youth—that accumulation of hours, days, months and years, rises up before him and crushes him with its terrible weight. In order to be able to answer the critic—in four sessions—the poet has had to think and think for many hours. And it was in the early hours of the night that he would think, as he recalled his childhood and his youth, while in the darkness the waves advanced and receded upon the sand along the beach.

Felix talks now to Plácida about his past:

"What a world of agonizing recollections!" Felix exclaims. And he adds:

"For me the past is usually a black chaos, a dark void. I do not wish to see anything in it; for me it is pleasant not to focus upon anything in my past; in this way I have the feeling of always being young, of always looking upon life as new. And my work, since I am always engrossed in it with my entire personality, is more pleasant, more easily done, and more creative."

Plácida, standing there majestically, listens to the poet, her poet; their friendship is quite recent. The lady's pink, plump hand rests like a flower upon the white pages of the book.

And the poet adds:

"These past few days I have had to recall my childhood. And I saw it all, all of it, with dazzling clarity. When I make the slightest effort to probe into the past, a light suddenly flashes on in my brain and dispels the darkness, the pleasant, prolific darkness. I saw it all, Plácida. But do you know what I could not see clearly?"

Felix Vargas stops, and Plácida directs at him, at those eyes of a poet and dreamer, a fond, maternal look.

The poet continues:

"Do you see those children playing on the beach? Just watch them; they run and jump, take each other by the hand, and walk along in a line . . . Look at those two, a boy and a girl. Do you see them? There they are, in front of that mound of sand; he has a stick in his hand. Well, at one time I was like those children . . . Yes, I have been on this very beach in my childhood, just like that boy, accompanied by a girl like that one. There were ten or twelve of us who were friends; we used to play on the sand every day. And once I found myself a sweetheart; she was my fiancée for three or four days . . . the engagement lasted only that long. As a token of eternal love—yes, eternal love—she gave me a little periwinkle shell, and I gave her one exactly like it. Yesterday, while I was looking through a drawer for some papers, I found that little shell. And what a thrill that discovery gave me! I am going inside to get it; you shall see it."

Felix Vargas rose quickly, went into the house, and brought out the shell.

"What I should like to know," the poet added, "is the identity of that little girl who exchanged this token of eternal love with me. I met so many little girls during those years of my childhood! I haven't the slightest idea who she is. And what I wouldn't give to see her now, a grown woman, after all these years!"

Plácida looked at the poet in silence. For a moment her cheeks glowed a vivid red, and her eyes shone with a mysterious light. And as she was leaving she said:

"Felix, I want you to come to my house. Will you? The day after tomorrow. We must have a talk. I shall be waiting for you."

Two days later Felix Vargas went to see Plácida. The poet's excitement was intense. For a moment he had been standing there motionless, undecided, his gaze fixed upon Plácida's soft blue eyes. In his hand the poet had a little shell exactly like the one she was holding—the same black spots on the edge of each, the one held by Felix and the one held by Plácida.

"You, Plácida? You?" the poet was saying. "Were you . . . are you . . . that little girl? What tremendous coincidences there are in this world! I cannot, Plácida, I simply cannot say what I feel. Words fail me. . . ."

And Plácida's hand, so plump, so pink, so soft, rested for a moment maternally, lovingly, upon the poet's brow.

/Night. Outside, darkness. In the darkness, up the coast, the lighthouse beam that flashes, disappears, and flashes again./And the soothing sound of the waves, heard as well from Plácida's little house. The lady is seated at the table beneath the wide circle of the lamp's bright light. With her is her faithful, quiet maid, Tomasita. All is serenity and silence. Through the wide-open window the glittering stars can be seen shining in the vast, dark vault above.

"In truth," Plácida is saying in her sweet and solemn voice, "in truth, Tomasita, we have done well. What worry and work it was! I thought we were never going to find one. How we rushed about! But the little shell is the same, exactly the same, as the one belonging to Don Felix, with its little black spots. . . ."

Vicente Blasco Ibáñez (1867–1928)

. . . was, during his lifetime, the Spanish novelist best known outside his native country, due largely to his two novels that supported the cause of the Allies during World War I—*The Four Horsemen of the Apocalypse* (1916) and *Mare Nostrum* (1918), both of which were made into motion pictures in Hollywood and reached a world-wide audience. His novel against bullfighting, *Blood and Sand* (1908), was also made into a motion picture. The fact that Rudolf Valentino and Tyrone Power starred in his films was of no little assistance in popularizing the name of Blasco Ibáñez. These novels, however, were not his best by any means.

His finest works are his earlier ones, which deal with the Mediterranean region of Valencia; his masterpiece is undoubtedly *The Cabin* (1898). It describes the social and economic conflicts between the peasants and landowners of the subtropical, irrigated Valencian countryside.

Blasco Ibáñez' works were extremely popular with the general public in Spain and abroad. (*The Four Horsemen of the Apocalypse,* for example, went through more than two hundred printings in English alone.) But he did not fare well at the hands of the literary critics: his novels—especially the later ones—were too hastily written, and he never corrected anything he wrote. His personal vigor and intensity carried over into his writing.

He was a stormy political and social reformer, constantly concerned with the problems of the peasants and workers. He was often jailed for the political views he expressed in radical journals and in street demonstrations. After some years spent in Argentina, he returned to Spain and again took up his campaign for reform. He was elected eight times to the Spanish parliament. Because of his opposition to the monarchy and to the dictatorship of Primo de Rivera, he went into exile in France, where he died at the expensive villa on the Côte d'Azur which he had bought with the money earned from the film rights to his novels. To the end he kept fulminating against King Alfonso XIII in articles and pamphlets.

Blasco Ibáñez was especially well acquainted with the fisherfolk of the seaport of Valencia, where he was born. Many of his best short stories, like the one translated here, deal with the sea and the hard life of the Valencians who wrest a precarious living from fishing or from coastwise shipping.

Man Overboard!

THE CATBOAT *San Rafael* left Torrevieja at nightfall with a cargo of salt for Gibraltar. The hold was loaded to capacity, and bags were piled on the deck in a mound around the mainmast. To pass from the bow to the stern the crew had to walk along the gunwales, balancing themselves precariously.

The night was calm—a summer night, with myriad stars scattered in the sky. There was a fresh, variable breeze which would alternately fill the triangular sail until the mast creaked, and then stop blowing suddenly, causing the enormous canvas to fall limp with a loud flap.

The crew—five men and a boy—ate supper after maneuvering the boat out of the harbor. From captain to cabin boy they all dipped their dry bread into the steaming pot with seafaring fellowship, and when it was empty all those who were off duty went below to rest on the hard, thin mattress with their stomachs full of wine and watermelon juice.

Old man Chispas took his trick at the wheel. He was a toothless old sea dog who accepted the captain's final instructions with growls of impatience. Next to him stood his protégé Juanillo, a beginner who making his first sea voyage in the *San Rafael*. The youth was very grateful to the old man, thanks to whom he had been signed on as a crew member, thus overcoming his not inconsiderable hunger. To him, the old catboat seemed like an admiral's flagship, an enchanted bark sailing on a sea of abundance.

That night's supper was the first real one he had ever eaten in his life. He had grown to the age of nineteen, hungry and almost as naked as a savage, in the rickety shack where his rheumatic grandmother— an invalid—moaned and prayed. He slept there at night, and by day he helped to launch boats, unloaded baskets of fish, or went along as an extra hand on boats that fished for tuna or sardines so he could bring home a few small fish. But now, thanks to old man Chispas, who was good to him because he had known the boy's father, he could dip his hand into the pot quite rightfully. He was even wearing shoes for the first time in his life, splendid pieces of workmanship, as seaworthy as a frigate; he adored them ecstatically. And then people say the things they do about going to sea! Bah! It was the best life in the world!

Old man Chispas, without taking his eyes off the prow or his hands off the helm, and crouching down in order to peer between the sail and the mound of bags ahead into the darkness, was listening to him with a sly smile.

"Yes; you haven't chosen a bad trade, but it has its drawbacks. You'll see, by the time you reach my age . . . But your place isn't here. Get up in the bow, and sing out if you see a boat ahead of us."

Juanillo ran along the gunwale with the calm confidence of a boy brought up by the seashore.

"Careful, boy, careful!"

But he was already up in the bow. He sat down near

the boom and scanned the black surface of the sea, upon which the flickering stars were reflected in shimmering streaks of light. The catboat, broad and heavy laden, dropped down from each wave crest with a resounding *plop!* which made drops of water splash up into Juanillo's face. Sheets of phosphorescent foam slipped by on either side of the broad bow, and the swelling sail, its tall top lost in the darkness, seemed to scrape the vault of heaven.

What king or admiral was better off than the forward watch on the *San Rafael?* Brrp! His full stomach belched with satisfaction. This was the life!

"Chispas! Have you got a cigar?"

"Come and get it!"

Juanillo ran along the gunwale on the side away from the wind. There was a momentary calm, and the sail flapped and fluttered as it started to fall limp against the mast. But a breeze sprang up, and the boat heeled over with a sudden lurch. Juanillo, in order to keep his balance, clutched the edge of the sail, which at that very instant bellied out as if it were about to split apart. The catboat lunged forward with a burst of speed, and the sail swelled against the young man's whole body with such irresistible force that it hurtled him overboard as if from a catapult.

As Juanillo was swallowed by the waves he thought he heard a cry; the words were lost in the noise and confusion; perhaps it was the old helmsman who was shouting:

"Man overboard!"

He went down deep—very deep—stunned by the blow and by the surprising suddenness of his fall. Almost before he realized it he was at the surface again, thrashing his arms and gasping down gulps of cool air

. . . And the boat? It was already out of sight. The sea was very dark, much darker than it seemed from the deck of the catboat.

He thought he could make out a white smudge floating phantom-like on the waves in the distance, and he swam toward it. Then suddenly he didn't see it there, but in the opposite direction; he turned about, lost, swimming strongly but without knowing where he was going. His shoes weighed like lead. Curse them! And the first time he was wearing them! His cap was cutting into his temples; his pants were pulling him down as if they reached the bottom of the sea and were dragging in the seaweed.

"Don't panic, Juanillo, don't panic."

And he threw away his cap, regretting that he could not do the same with his shoes.

He was a good swimmer, and felt confident that he could last for two hours. The boat would come about, and the crew would pick him up; a good soaking, that was all . . . so what? Anyway, men don't just die like this, do they? In a storm, yes . . . the way his father and grandfather had died . . . but on a beautiful night like this, in a calm sea, to die because you were pushed overboard by a sail would be ridiculous. He swam on and on, always thinking he saw that phantom which kept changing its position, and waiting for the *San Rafael* to loom up in the darkness looking for him.

"Ship ahoy! Chispas! Captain!"

But shouting tired him, and two or three times the waves filled his mouth. Curse them! From the boat they seemed so insignificant, but out there in the water, submerged as far as his neck and forced to move his arms continually in order to keep himself afloat, they kept choking him as they buffeted him about in their noiseless swell and opened their gaping, moving mouths that closed up quickly as if to swallow him.

He kept thinking, but with a certain amount of uneasiness, about his two hours of endurance. Yes, he was counting on them; for two hours and more he used to swim tirelessly at his beach. But that was during daylight, and in crystal-clear blue water through whose remarkable transparency he could see deep down to the yellow rocks festooned with sharp-pointed marine plants extending like branches of green coral; and below were pink conch-shells, pearl-colored starfish, and luminous flowers with fleshy petals that rippled as they were brushed by silver-bellied fishes. But now he was out on the pitch-black sea, lost in the darkness and weighted down by his clothing; and below there were Heaven knows how many wrecked ships, how many corpses stripped of flesh by voracious fishes! He shivered when his wet pants rubbed against him, imagining that he felt the touch of sharp teeth.

Tired and faint, he turned over on his back and let himself be borne along by the waves. The taste of his supper rose in his throat. Accursed meal, and at what a cost he had earned it! He would probably end up by drowning out there foolishly . . . But the instinct of self-preservation made him straighten up. Perhaps they were looking for him, and if he were lying flat they might pass by without seeing him. Back to swimming again, driven by desperation. On the crests of the waves he would raise himself up in order to see a greater distance, and would swim first in one direction, then another, always churning about in the same circle.

They were abandoning him as if he were a rag that had fallen off the boat. My God! Is that the way a man is forgotten? It couldn't be . . . Perhaps they were looking for him at that very moment. A boat goes fast; no matter how quickly they had come up on deck and struck sail, they were probably a mile off by now. And as he was cherishing this illusion, he started sinking slowly as if someone were pulling him down by his heavy shoes. In his mouth he tasted the bitter salt . . . it blinded his eyes . . . the waters closed over his close-cropped head . . . But a little whirlpool formed between two waves, a pair of clutching hands emerged, and he came to the surface.

His arms were growing numb, and his head slumped over on his chest as if drooping in sleep. It seemed to Juanillo that the sky had changed: the stars were red, like blotches of blood. The sea no longer frightened him; he felt a desire to lie back on the water and rest.

He remembered his grandmother, who was probably thinking about him at just this time. And he tried to pray, as he had heard the poor old woman do a thousand times. "Our Father, who art in Heaven . . ." He was praying silently, but without realizing it his tongue moved and he said in a voice so hoarse that it seemed to belong to someone else:

"The swine! The crooks! They are abandoning me!"

He was going down again . . . he disappeared as he fought in vain to stay afloat . . . someone was pulling him down by his shoes . . . He went down in the darkness, swallowing water, stiff, exhausted . . . but without knowing how, he came to the surface again. Now the stars were black, darker than the sky, and stood out like blots of ink.

He was finished. This time he would really go to the bottom: his body felt like lead. He went under, pulled straight down by his new shoes. And as he sank deep into the abyss of rotting ships and fleshless skeletons, his brain, swirling around and around in a dense cloud, kept repeating:

"Our Father . . . Our Father . . . The crooks! The scoundrels! They have abandoned me!"

Alfredo Marquerie (1907–   )

. . . was born in the Balearic Islands, which lie off the Mediterranean coast of Spain. They were annexed to Spain in the thirteenth century by James I of Catalonia, who wrested them from Moorish control. The islands have always had a linguistic bond with Barcelona, capital of Catalonia, and with Valencia, the city of El Cid. Most young men from the Balearics go to either of those two cities for their university education, where Catalán and its kindred Valencian tongue are spoken; Castilian Spanish is used only as the official language. For this reason, few writers from the eastern seaboard of Spain find their way into the mainstream of Spanish literature. (Blasco Ibáñez was an exception, and even his writings are studded with Valencian words and phrases, particularly in his regional works.) But in Catalonia there is a considerable body of fine literature in their own Romance tongue.

Alfredo Marquerie, however, had his preparatory schooling in Segovia, which is in Old Castile, and then went to Madrid to study law. He took his doctor's degree in that discipline, but decided on a literary rather than a legal career. Perhaps because Marquerie was not born on the mainland he has a more detached point of view, and can focus more clearly upon the problems and foibles of peninsular Spain. Critics have said the same of Spain's greatest modern novelist, Pérez Galdós, who was born in the Canary Islands.

As a journalist, essayist and writer of short stories, Marquerie has contributed to his country's best newspapers, magazines and literary reviews. He has also been a theater critic on the staff of one of Madrid's leading dailies, and has held a managerial position on another.

His published works to date total more than twenty volumes. The selection translated here was published in Madrid in an anthology of the best Spanish short stories. Its locale could be any large city in present-day Spain; the "islands" mentioned are, no doubt, Marquerie's native Balearics. But it is the universality of the tale and of the protagonist's plight that gives it an international appeal.

Self-Service Elevator

HE HAD OPENED the elevator door to let the young lady enter first, but he could not get a clear view of her face. Once inside that vertical vehicle's community cloister he asked the question which has become almost a ritual:

"What floor?"

He pressed the button, and the elevator started up. In situations like this Luis was always conscious of a strange sensation. A chance encounter with a woman in this kind of captive balloon gave him a sort of anxiety state. "Here"—he would say to himself—"is a case of unavoidable and enforced intimacy. Two people who perhaps have never seen or spoken to each other, and who may separate afterwards and never meet again for all eternity, live together face to face for a few moments in a cramped cubicle, prying into each other's lives even in spite of themselves, because in the brief time the trip lasts they have nothing else to do but to stare and to theorize about one another."

But on that occasion Luis had, from the very beginning, the distinct feeling that the girl with whom he was sharing the little lift was clearly not a stranger. With a single glance his mind had registered admiration of her taste in clothes: two solid colors—the maroon of her tailored suit and the green of her gloves, hat, purse and shoes—made his quick evaluation easier and faster. In a moment, then, it was possible for him to devote his glances to her face, which was as smooth as porcelain and had lips like fresh red fruit. Her thin eyebrows arched over a pair of dark eyes that contrasted with her long, natural-blonde hair, light as honey and fine as spun gold.

"Where have I seen this dark-eyed blonde before?" he began to wonder.

The girl was not paying the slightest attention to Luis. She seemed preoccupied or lost in thought, and she had a far-away, diamond-like sheen in her unseeing eyes.

Luis' whole thought-process had been more than fast: it had been fleeting, not more than a few seconds in duration. Before he reached the first floor he was sure he knew his chance travelling companion.

Suddenly the elevator jerked to a halt. They hadn't reached the second floor, and through the glass in the door they could see the wall and the elevator cables.

"What happened?" asked the dark-eyed blonde.

The tone and inflection of her voice as she asked the question enabled him to identify the young lady and to place her precisely in a definite period of his youthful past. Luis was delighted with his discovery, and rejoiced inwardly at this identification, as one usually does when relieved of the almost physical torture of knowing someone without being quite able to place him. This inner satisfaction kept him from answering her question immediately, kept him from returning to reality so he could pay attention to what was happening and to what she was saying. Finally, after realizing that the elevator had suddenly stopped, he answered stupidly:

"Well, you can see: this old crate has stopped."

"What can the trouble be?"

Luis, glad of the mishap that had given him a pretext for conversation, shrugged his shoulders and replied, "I don't know. A power failure, maybe. Or else somebody has opened a door. I'm going to try something."

He went to press one of the buttons, but the girl made a timid, frightened gesture and stopped him with her gloved hand: "No! Please!"

"Are you afraid?"

"Suppose we drop down all of a sudden?"

"Oh, no! I'm going to press the up-button."

He tried several, but the elevator didn't budge. He smiled soothingly: "Nothing happened, you see?"

"Yes, but we're not moving."

"Now let's see. I'm going to press the emergency button."

The electric alarm in the box on the staircase clanged loud and long. From below came the thick voice of the porter, like a great glob from a gushing spout:

"What's the matter?"

Putting his mouth near the crack in the door, Luis replied, "We're stuck between floors!"

The voice from the ground floor counselled caution: "Don't open the door. I'm going to try the down-button."

The preliminary click sounded clearly, but the elevator did not start down.

The girl commented: "This is not funny at all."

Luis seemed quite amused by the incident, and the comment was no doubt intended to reproach him for the satisfaction betrayed by his ill-concealed smile.

They heard the wheezing porter pant up the steps one by one, and heard him try the buttons on each floor without success. Finally, from the very top of the staircase came this almost sensational announcement:

"The cables have come loose and are twisted. There is no danger, understand, but you'll have to wait a while. I'm going to put in an emergency call."

The girl's ashen face no longer showed annoyance or distress, but sheer panic. With contorted features and wide-opened eyes, and her mouth twisted into a frightened grimace, she uttered just three syllables:

"Oh, my God!" And then she crossed herself devoutly.

Luis felt himself obliged to calm her, and to try to restore her peace of mind. He began to bring into play all kinds of arguments, and to employ his most persuasive tone of voice:

"Come on, now; just calm down! Please don't worry. This happens lots of times."

"But won't we crash down?"

"Heavens, no! You heard what he said; it's just that the cables are tangled."

"Now what will be done?"

"Well, they'll come and untangle them."

"Will they be long?"

Luis consulted his wrist watch gravely, like a doctor taking someone's pulse: "Fifteen minutes to get here, another fifteen to get us out . . . It's two o'clock now . . . We should be free by half past two."

"You sound as though we were in jail!"

"Well, we certainly are imprisoned here."

"I should say so! I'm furious!"

"Furious? Why?"

"Surely this can't seem pleasant to you?"

"This mishap has given me the great pleasure of your company."

"This isn't exactly the occasion for compliments."

"Quite to the contrary, I believe that a case like this, or one similar to it—a fire or a shipwreck, for example— is precisely where one can reveal his good upbringing.

In that connection, let me tell you a story about. . . ."

"This is no time for stories! Appealing to your good upbringing, I beg you to. . . ."

Luis made a gesture like a good man wronged, and then said jokingly:

"Señorita, please! Aren't you forgetting that you are in my power, and that even though you may scream at the top of your lungs nobody can come to help you? Believe me, if this hadn't happened by accident, I'd have arranged it with the greatest of pleasure. This is a trick for catching dark-eyed little blondes that I intend to begin putting into practice with the help of my porter friends."

"It certainly is quite a scheme!"

"Come, now! Are you still worried and nervous?"

"Do you think I should start dancing for joy?"

"But could you tell me the reason for your displeasure, aside from the delay involved?"

"That's very simple. First of all, the danger. . . ."

"There isn't any. The service men will come and raise the elevator easily."

"Then, I'm going to be late at the office."

"Let them know."

"How?"

"By calling to the porter. Use your wireless telephone, the good old voice system that I used before."

At that instant Luis suddenly remembered her name: Alba Vélez. And to surprise her, he shouted loudly: "Hey, porter! Señorita Alba Vélez wants you to. . . ."

She stifled a startled cry: "Oh! You know me?"

". . . tell her office that she's been kidnapped and is being held prisoner in this elevator!"

Then, turning to the girl and making an exaggerated,

mock-heroic bow, he explained: "Of course I know you. I've known you for many years."

"From the islands, perhaps?" [1]

"Exactly right."

"Do you come from there?"

"No, but I lived there for a while, quite near your house."

"In the capital?"

"Naturally."

"But I don't remember you."

It occurred to Luis that for a joke, just to make the half-hour's wait in the elevator amusing, he should give a false name. He said:

"My name is Dámaso Jelez."

"I still don't remember you."

"I've often met you and your sisters."

"The poor girls are dead now."

"I'm truly sorry."

There were a few painful moments of silence. Alba finally renewed the conversation:

"'I'm alone now, and working. But tell me: with whom did you used to associate there in the islands?"

The joke could be kept going on its merry way with surprising complications and digressions: Alba didn't recognize him. Luis could have some unexpected fun by playing with his own real name, so he said:

"I used to go around with Luis Martín."

"Oh, that fellow! I remember him, all right!" she exclaimed.

"What ever became of him?" asked the real Luis with the most innocent expression in the world.

[1] These could be the Balearics, where the author was born, or the Canary Islands.

"Bah! He's a hopeless case, a crackpot, a scoundrel."

When he heard this revelation he felt an irrepressible urge to interrupt such insults, and was on the point of shouting, "Be careful, there! I'm Luis Martín!" But he succeeded in restraining himself. The expression of alarm and surprise on his face made her suspect something, however.

Alba said, "Are you still a friend of his?"

Luis reacted quickly, and dissembled:

"Who, me? I don't know a thing about the fellow. But where do you get your information?"

"Oh, from friends of his, and from his sister."

"From my . . . from his friends?"

Alba became talkative. She decided to sit down on the still-motionless elevator's red velvet-covered bench. Luis did the same. The girl continued talking, more and more confidentially:

"You see, Luis Martín's sister is a very good family friend, and she always keeps us posted on his activities. Luis is a young man with absolutely no stability or steadfastnesss of purpose. Women laugh at him, and have fooled him frightfully. He just throws his money away. First he's riding high, then he's absolutely broke. He has tried I don't know how many lines of business: automobiles, radio . . . he prefers modern things. But he always makes a mess of it. His friends say he's a lunatic, that he tires of everything right away, and that he is incapable of being serious about anything. Occasionally luck is with him, and he makes some money. But as soon as he has to pay steady attention to what he's doing, he's hopelessly lost."

The points that Alba was making, while essentially true, contained such distortions of the facts and were

such an unkind caricature of his life that Luis felt
obliged to protest:

"That's not what I hear."

"Oh, no?"

"'The information that reaches me through friends is
that Luis has indeed tried several lines of business, some
with good results and others which were less fortunate.
But I don't believe he is an unstable person; he is a
man who gets involved in very complicated business
activities and therefore he sometimes succeeds and sometimes fails. Now, as to women. . . .'"

Alba interrupted: "About that point everyone is in
agreement. Surely you're not going to defend him? Not
only does his sister say so, but also Alicia, a girl from
our part of the country . . . you may know her. . . ."

"Yes, slightly."

"Well, she was engaged to Martín and can tell you
what a laugh she had at his expense. She had another
boy friend at the same time, and Luis never even caught
on at all: he believed every excuse she gave him as if it
were Gospel truth. And I don't know how many things
he bought for her: wrist watches, pocketbooks,
dresses . . . Then one day she pretended to be angry
because he came late, and they broke off the engagement. 'This simpleton Luis,' she said, 'has been buying
me my whole trousseau.' What a laugh we had!"

Luis thought about Alicia, and not even by recalling
very carefully the details of his foolish engagement
could he recollect that cruel trick. But the facts were
true, without a doubt. Through the medium of his
joke he was coming to some startling and unsuspected
conclusions about the world and himself. He pressed on,
morbidly:

"And you say that his sister. . . ."

"Oh, his sister is the one who has the worst opinion of him. Of course, he helps her financially, but here is how she puts it: 'What's the difference if he's generous with me? He spends so much on other people . . . Basically, it isn't pity that I feel for him: it's scorn.'"

Inwardly Luis made a firm resolve to hold his sister to a strict accounting for such slanderous remarks. But together with this desire for vengeance came a special uneasiness. He would never have thought that people—his own family and outsiders—had such an opinion of him. He could never have imagined the existence of such ideas about himself, nor that these ideas were in such general circulation. He fell silent, and began to think: "Yes, indeed; we certainly don't know ourselves. Can we really be as others see us? In fact, if I hadn't tried this experiment of hiding my identity, and if I hadn't asked the questions I did, I should have gone on to my dying day without knowing what other people were thinking of me. And wouldn't I have been happier not knowing? I wonder how many others have had this same experience? We are deceived by those around us. We don't believe what our enemies say about us because their opinions are lowered or biased by envy or hate; nor can we give any weight to what friends state in our presence, because personal considerations and flattery usually twist the truth. But what my friends and my sister are saying must be true. I have never seen myself in such a clear, hard mirror; it had never occurred to me to listen behind closed doors. I must be—I am—'that fellow' Alba described, but in another incarnation, different and distinct from the one I had supposed."

"You've fallen very quiet and thoughtful. What's the matter?" said Alba.

Martín tried to cover up: "Could you believe it? I've caught your fear of a possible sudden fall of this cage we're stuck in."

"Oh, you said 'possible' fall."

"Now don't get nervous again. There is no such possibility."

"Then why did that word slip out?"

"How do I know? I probably meant something else; I must have been absorbed in my thoughts."

"I, too, was thinking of our conversation about Martín. The subject isn't really worth it, though. At least it's been a good excuse for a chat."

Swallowing his deep chagrin with great difficulty, Martín felt obliged to say: "It wasn't necessary to fall back on any pretext in order to spend a delightful moment talking with you."

"Very gallant."

"But listen! Here come our rescuers!"

On the staircase could be heard the steps of the service men going up to straighten out the cables and repair the elevator. Alba clapped her hands joyfully:

"This has all the thrill of an episode in a book or an adventure film. I remember a novel in which a girl was being saved from a fire, and the chapter that described the moment when the firemen appeared at the window sill among the smoke and flames."

"You have quite an imagination."

"Perhaps less than other girls my age. But with to-day's incident I now have something to tell about."

The cable pulleys creaked overhead, and after a few unsuccessful starts the elevator rose with two sudden jerks until it reached the floor level. Alba hardly realized it.

Martín said simply: "We're there!"

Alba sighed: "Good! That wasn't so bad, thank Heaven."

He opened the door, and went out into the hall after the young lady. Holding out his hand, he said: "Friends?"

"I should say so! And thanks for the chat; without you I'd have died of fright."

Smiling happily, Alba went up the staircase with bird-like little hops, and was soon lost to view beyond the first landing.

Martín stayed where he was for a while, standing next to the door of the elevator from which he had emerged—as if reborn—into a strange new world, to an unusual understanding of his own personality, to a rediscovery of himself.

"Am I the same man as before?" he wondered. No more than a few minutes separated him from 'before,' but Luis understood why it is said that there are minutes that count as centuries, that have the function, value and meaning of eternity. A man can have two lives, one unknown, the other recently discovered . . .

He summed up his ideas with the thought: "How young I am! I have just been born!"

Mariano José de Larra (1809–1837)

    . . . was born into troubled times in Spain. The Napoleonic invasion was followed by the bloody War of Independence (so graphically depicted in Goya's etchings), and then came the despotism of Ferdinand VII until 1833. Small wonder that Larra, a sensitive Liberal, was disillusioned by the failure of the dream of democracy in his day, and became deeply pessimistic like so many of his fellow Romantics in Spain and the rest of Europe. A troubled personal life added fuel to the fire: he had married at twenty, but his marriage was a failure. He turned to an old flame, who had since married. She broke off their relationship. Embittered, he saw his country in collapse and his life in ruins.

He was a newspaperman, and wrote a famous article at the end of the year 1836: *All Soul's Day: Figaro in the Cemetery*. In it he viewed Madrid as a vast burial ground where liberty, national credit and political sanity lay entombed. The names on the public buildings were nothing but inscriptions on mausoleums. Then he looked into his own heart: "My heart is just another sepulchre. What does it say on it? Who lies dead in here? Frightful inscription! 'Here lies hope!'" Shortly afterward he shot himself, and Spain lost one of her greatest prose writers. He was twenty-eight years old.

Larra's father was a Madrid doctor who had fled to France in 1814, taking his family with him. When the boy returned to Madrid at the age of eight, he could speak only in French. He learned Spanish at school, and after his education ended he entered the field of journalism at the age of nineteen. Soon famous for his ironic articles on the fads and foibles of Madrid society, he took several pseudonyms, the best-known of which was Figaro. His sketches of customs in the capital are witty and mordant. With unerring accuracy he depicts his country's faults, and though he smiles outwardly he suffers deep inside. "To write in Madrid," he says, "is to weep."

Larra was greatly attracted by the tale of the fifteenth-century Galician troubadour Macías, who died for love of a married woman, a situation that paralleled his own tragic love affair. He wrote a play and a novel on this Romantic

119

theme. He was also a drama critic of great renown in his day, and his articles of literary criticism are a fertile field for the study of the Romantic movement in Spain. But it is his collection of articles on Spanish customs that places him in the forefront of the great prose writers of the nineteenth century. The best of these are contained in a collection published in 1832–1833; they are as true today as when they were written more that a century ago. It is from this group of articles, written in a lighter vein but presaging his pessimism, that the following typical selection is translated.

Come Back Tomorrow

THE FIRST man who called laziness a mortal sin must have been a great person. We, who were more serious in one of our preceding articles than we ever intended to be, will not enter now upon a long and profound discussion of the history of this sin, however much we may realize that there are sins that border on the historical and that the history of sin would be rather intriguing. Let us agree to say only that laziness has closed—and will continue to close—the gates of Heaven to more than one Christian.

I happened to be thinking along these lines a few days ago, when there appeared at my house one of those foreigners who, for good or ill, must always have exaggerated ideas about our country—one of those who believe either that men here are still the splendid, generous, frank and chivalrous *caballeros* they were in the seventeenth century, or else that they are still nomadic tribesmen from beyond the Atlas Mountains in North Africa. In the first case, they keep imagining that our national character has been conserved intact, like our ruins; in the second, they go trembling along the roads and asking whether the members of some military unit established specifically to protect them from the hazards of the highway—common to all countries—are brigands out to despoil them.

The truth is that our country is not one of those that you can get to know at first—or even at second—sight. And if we were not afraid of being called bold we might easily compare it to one of those feats of leger-demain which are surprising and unfathomable to one who does not know the trick (usually based upon the merest trifle) and which, after it is known, leaves the very one who was racking his brains looking for weird explanations astonished at his lack of observation. Many times the lack of an obvious cause of things makes us believe that it must be deep to be hidden from our penetrating mind. Such is the pride of man, who would rather declare in a loud voice that some-thing is incomprehensible if he cannot understand it, than to confess that his ignorance of it may be the result of his own mental sluggishness. Despite this, and because there are many of us Spaniards who are really ignorant of our basic characteristics, we have no right to think it strange that foreigners cannot understand us easily.

It was one of these foreigners who came to my house bearing proper letters of recommendation addressed to me. Complicated family matters, legal claims to be made, and even vast plans thought up in Paris about investing his abundant capital here in some industrial or business venture, were the motives that brought him to our country.

Accustomed to the active pace of our northern neighbors, he assured me seriously that he intended to remain here a very short time, especially if he did not soon find something safe in which to invest his money. It seemed to me that this foreigner was worthy of consideration, and I quickly made friends with him. Full of pity, I tried to persuade him to go home right away if the object of his visit was anything except a vacation. He was astonished at my suggestion, and I had to explain myself more clearly.

I said to him, "Look, Monsieur Sans-Délai," for this was his name, "you have decided to spend two weeks here to settle your affairs?"

"Certainly," he answered me. "Two weeks will be more than enough. Tomorrow morning we look up a genealogist to take care of my family affairs; in the afternoon he searches through his books for my ancestors, and by evening I find out who I am. As for my claims of an inheritance, the day after tomorrow I present them, based on the genealogist's data, notarized in compliance with the law; and as it will be a clear-cut case of undeniable justice (since only thus will I assert my rights), on the third day the matter is up for judgment, and I have my property. As for the business venture in which I intend to invest my capital, on the fourth day I shall present my proposals; these may be good or bad, and accepted or rejected immediately, and that makes five days. On the sixth, seventh and eighth days I see the sights in Madrid. On the ninth, I rest. On the tenth day, I take my seat on the stage coach if I do not feel like spending more time here, and I return to my home. I still have five days left over."

When M. Sans-Délai reached this point, I tried to repress a laugh that had been about to split my sides for some time. My upbringing succeeded in stifling my untimely mirth, but it was unable to prevent a slight smile of astonishment and pity from springing to my lips, brought there against my will by his efficient plans.

"Permit me, Monsieur Sans-Délai," I said to him half in jest and half in earnest, "permit me to invite you to dine with me on the day you have spent fifteen months in Madrid."

"What do you mean?"

"You will still be here in Madrid fifteen months from now."

"Are you joking?"

"Certainly not!"

"I shall not be able to leave here when I please? The idea strikes me as very funny indeed!"

"You should realize that you are not in your bustling, businesslike country."

"Ah, you Spaniards who have travelled abroad have acquired the habit of speaking ill of your country so that you can feel superior to your compatriots."

"I assure you that during the two weeks you are planning to devote to these matters, you will not even be able to speak to a single one of the people whose cooperation you need."

"What exaggeration! My energy will rub off on all of them."

"Their inertia will rub off on you!"

I realized that M. Sans-Délai was in no mood to be convinced except by experience, so I kept still for the moment, quite sure that the facts would soon bear me out.

Very early the next day we went out together to look for a genealogist, which could be done only by asking one friend or acquaintance after another. Finally we found one, and the good man, stunned by our haste, declared frankly that he needed some time for this; we pressed him, and he finally told us as a great favor that we should come around in a few days. I smiled, and we left. Three days passed, and we returned.

"Come back tomorrow," the maid told us. "The master is not up yet."

"Come back tomorrow," she told us the next day. "The master has just gone out."

"Come back tomorrow," she said on the following day. "The master is taking his siesta."

"Come back tomorrow," she answered the next Monday. "Today he has gone to the bullfight."

At what time can one see a Spaniard?

Finally we saw him.

"Come back tomorrow," he told us, "because I have forgotten the document."

"Come back tomorrow, because the final copy needs touching up."

At the end of two weeks it was ready. But M. Sans-Délai had asked him for a report on the name Díez, while he had understood my French friend to say Díaz, and the information was of no use. While waiting for new evidence I said nothing to my friend, who was now in despair about ever learning about his family tree. Obviously, without this as a basis his legal claims were groundless.

For the proposals he brought concerning several very useful business enterprises that he intended to establish, it was necessary to find a translator. With the translator we had to go through the same rigamarole as with the genealogist: what with one "mañana" after another, it took us until the end of the month. We discovered that the translator was urgently in need of money, even for his daily meals, but he never found that the time was right for working. The office clerk was the same about making copies of the translation, for there just aren't any copyists in this country who know how to write well.

And matters did not stop there. A tailor took twenty days to make him a coat which he had promised within twenty-four hours. The bootmaker, with all his dallying, obliged my friend to buy a ready-made pair. The laundress took two weeks to wash and iron a dress shirt for him, and the hatter, to whom he had sent his hat for a slight adjustment of the brim, kept it for two days, so he could not go out of the house—unless he went bareheaded.

His friends and acquaintances did not show up for a single appointment, failed to notify him when they could not come, and did not reply to his inquiries. What manners! What punctuality!

"What do you think of this country now, Monsieur Sans-Délai?" I asked him when these proofs of my opinion became evident.

"It seems to me that these men are rather un-usual. . . ."

"Well, that's the way they all are. They won't even eat, so as to avoid having to raise the food to their mouths."

In the course of time, however, he made a proposal to install improvements in a certain government department which I shall not name, since it is highly regarded. In four days we returned to learn whether our plan had been approved.

"Come back tomorrow," the doorman said. "The Chief Clerk did not come in today."

"Something very important must have detained him," I said to myself.

We went out for a walk in Retiro Park, and we met—

what a coincidence!—the Chief Clerk, very busy taking a stroll with his wife beneath the bright sun of Madrid's clear winter skies.

The next day was Tuesday, and the doorman said to us: "Come back tomorrow, because the Honorable Chief Clerk isn't seeing anyone today."

"Some very important business must have come up," I said.

And since I'm an impish devil, I sought an opportunity to look through the keyhole. His Honor was tossing a cigar butt into the fire, and had in his hand a puzzle from the *Daily Mail* which he must have been having some difficulty in solving.

"It is impossible to see him today," I said to my companion. "His Honor is indeed very busy."

The following Wednesday he granted us an interview, and—what a misfortune!—the document had been referred, unfortunately, to the only person opposed to the plan, because he was the one who would come out the loser. The document stayed under investigation for two months, and came back as well investigated as you might expect. The truth is that we had been unable to obtain any influence with a certain person who was very friendly with the investigator. This person had very pretty eyes which doubtless might have convinced him, during his free time, about the justice of our case.

When it came back from the investigation it suddenly dawned on the blessed office that that document did not belong in that department! This slight error had to be rectified: it went to the proper department, bureau and desk, and there we were after three months, still chasing our document around like a weasel chasing a rabbit, without being able to get it out of the hole dead or alive! It seems that at this point the document left the original office and never reached the other one.

In the first, they told us: "It left here on such-and-such a date."

And in the other they said: "It never reached us here."

"I swear!" I said to M. Sans-Délai. "Do you know, our document must be floating around in the air like a lost soul, and must now be perched like a pigeon on some roof in this busy town?"

We had to draw up another document. Back to the petitioning and the hurrying around! What a madhouse!

"It is absolutely necessary," said the official in a pompous voice, "that these matters go through regular channels."

That is to say, the requirement was—as in the army—that our document should spend so many years in the service. Finally, after almost six months of going upstairs and downstairs, waiting for signatures or for further investigation, or for approval, or to this office or that desk and always waiting for "mañana," it came back with a notation in the margin which said: "Despite the legality and usefulness of the proposal, petition denied."

"Ah, Monsieur Sans-Délai," I exclaimed, laughing loudly, "this is the way we handle things!"

But M. Sans-Délai, cursing all bureaucrats, flew into a towering rage:

"For this I took such a long journey? After six months, the only thing I have achieved is to have everyone everywhere say every day, 'Come back tomorrow.' And when this blessed 'tomorrow' finally arrives, they turn us down with a resounding negative! And I am here to invest money with them? And I am here to do them a favor? A very complex intrigue must be afoot to hinder our plans."

"An intrigue, Monsieur Sans-Délai? No man here is capable of staying with an intrigue for two consecutive hours. The real 'intrigue' is laziness. I assure you there is no other; that is the great, hidden motive: it is easier to deny something than to become informed about it."

At this point I should not like to leave unmentioned some of the reasons they gave me for the aforementioned denial of the petition, even though I may be digressing slightly:

"That man is going to bankrupt himself," a very serious and patriotic person told me.

"That's not the reason," I replied. "If he bankrupts himself, you will have lost nothing in granting him what he requests: he will suffer the consequences of his own recklessness or his ignorance."

"How will he succeed in his plans?"

"And suppose he wants to throw away his money and ruin himself? Can't a person even die around here without a permit from the Chief Clerk?"

"But he might harm those who have done in a different way the very things the foreign gentleman wants to do."

"Those who have done them differently? By that you mean they have done them less efficiently?"

"Yes, but at least they got them done!"

"What a pity it would be if things stopped being done badly! So then, because things have always been done in the worst possible way, must you be considerate of those who would perpetuate these inefficient methods? You might better consider whether old-fashioned people will harm up-to-date ones!"

"That is the regulation, that is the way things have been done until now, and that is the way we shall keep on doing them."

"By that token, you should still be fed baby-food as you were as an infant."

"After all, Señor Fígaro, he is a foreigner."

"Then why not have native Spaniards put his plan into operation?"

"That's just the kind of trick they use to bleed us of our money."

"My dear sir," I exclaimed, finally out of patience, "you are making an error that is all too widespread. You are like many others who have a diabolical mania for placing obstacles in the path of any good idea—and let someone just try to surmount them! Here in Spain we are madly proud of knowing nothing, of wanting to guess at everything, and of refusing to learn from masters. Nations without technical skill that have had the desire to acquire it, have found no better method than to turn to those who know more about these things.

"A foreigner," I continued, "who goes to an unfamiliar country to risk his capital there, puts new money into circulation and aids a society to which he is contributing his talent and his funds. If he meets failure, it is an heroic one; if he succeeds, it is quite proper that he should reap the reward of his efforts, since he is bringing us benefits we could not acquire by ourselves. A foreigner who sets up an establishment in this country is not coming to bleed us of our money, as you suppose; he must settle down here, and within a half-dozen years he is no longer a foreigner by any means: his dearest interests and his family bind him to his newly-adopted country. He comes to love the land in which he has made his fortune, and the people from whom he has perhaps chosen a wife; his children are Spanish, and his grandchildren will be Spaniards also. Instead of taking money out, he came and left capital that he brought with him, investing it and putting it to work. And he has left another kind of capital— talent, which is worth at least as much as money. He has provided a living for the native Spaniards he has had to employ, he has made improvements, and has even contributed toward an increase in the population with his new family. Convinced of these important truths, all wise and prudent governments have welcomed foreigners. France owes her high degree of prosperity to her great hospitality; Russia owes to foreigners from all the world the fact that she has become a great power in much less time than it has taken other nations to become so. The United States owes to its foreign immigration . . . But I see by your expression," I concluded, interrupting myself at an appropriate moment, "that it is very difficult to convince someone who has made up his mind not to be convinced. If you were in control of the government, we could certainly look forward to great things from you!"

And having delivered myself of this philippic, I went out to look for M. Sans-Délai.

"I am leaving, Señor Fígaro," he told me. "Nobody has any time in this country to attend to anything. I shall limit myself to seeing the most noteworthy things here in the capital."

"Ah, my friend," I said to him, "you had better leave in peace if you don't want to lose what little patience you still have left; the majority of our national treasures cannot be seen."

"Is that possible?"

"Aren't you ever going to believe me? Remember what I said about those fifteen days. . . ."

An expression on the face of M. Sans-Délai indicated that the recollection was an unpleasant one.

"Come back tomorrow," they told us everywhere, "because we have no visiting hours today. Fill out a slip so you can get special permission."

You should have seen my friend's face when he heard this about permission slips! In his mind's eye he was picturing the document, the petition, the six months, and . . . He said only:

"I am a foreigner."

A fine recommendation for my kind compatriots to hear! My friend became more and more bewildered, and understood us less and less. We had to wait days on end to see the few rare relics we have preserved.

Finally, after six long months (if there can be one six-month period longer than another) my protégé returned to his own country, cursing Spain and agreeing that I was correct in the first place. He took back with him excellent impressions of our customs: he said especially that all he had been able to do in six months was always to "come back tomorrow," and that at the end of all those "mañanas" that never came, the best thing—or, rather, the only good thing—he had been able to do was to leave the country.

Can he be right, leisurely reader (if you have reached this point in what I am writing), can the good M. Sans-Délai be right in speaking poorly of us and our laziness? Is it likely that he will return with pleasure the day after tomorrow to visit our homeland?

Let us leave this question for tomorrow, because you are probably tired of reading today; and if tomorrow, or some other day, you are not too lazy—as you usually are—to come back to the bookshop, too lazy to take out your purse, and too lazy to open your eyes to leaf through the pages I still have for you to read, I shall tell you how it happened (and I see and understand all this, and leave a lot untold) that I have many times, led by this same influence which is born of the climate and many other factors, lost out in more than one amorous adventure just because I was lazy; how I gave up more than one project I had begun, and the expectation of more than one job that would have been perhaps obtainable, if I had shown a little more activity; or how, in short, I gave up—just because I was too lazy to pay a call I owed or should have made—social connections that might have helped me a good deal during my life.

I shall confess to you that I do nothing today that can be put off until tomorrow; I shall tell you that I get up at eleven in the morning, and take a siesta in the afternoon; and that I spend seven and eight hours at a stretch loafing at a table in a café, talking—or snoring —like a good Spaniard. I shall add that when the café is closed I drag myself slowly to my daily appoint-ment (because out of lazinesss I make only one), and that I can be found glued to a chair smoking one cigarette after another and yawning continually until twelve or one o'clock in the morning; that many evenings I do not dine because I am too lazy, and that I am even too lazy to go to bed! In short, my dear reader, I shall state that despite the many times I have been in despair during my life, I have never hanged myself—and it was always due to sheer laziness.

Let me conclude for today by confessing that for more than three months I have had the title of this feature story—"Come Back Tomorrow"—at the head of a piece of notepaper, and that during this time I have wanted to write something on it every evening and many afternoons. But every night I would put out my light, promising myself with the most childish faith in my own willpower, "Ah, well, I'll write it tomorrow!"

Thank Heaven this "mañana" finally came, and it isn't too bad. But alas for that "mañana" that will never come!

Ramón de Mesonero Romanos (1803–1882)

. . . is the chronicler of his native Madrid. Like Larra, he was a creator of literary sketches about the customs of his city, but unlike that tragic young man his articles are full of good humor and mild reproof rather than mordant satire. Some of his works deal with the history of Madrid, political problems, and literary criticism, but the vast majority are devoted to short sketches about his favorite subject—the customs, costumes, fads and foibles of his beloved Madrid.

Some of the sketches by Mesonero Romanos appeared in literary reviews, others in a weekly magazine he himself founded in 1836. This was the apogee of Romanticism, and one of its elements was an intense interest in the folklore and customs of the people. With this nostalgic, sentimental antiquarianism Mesonero Romanos was in full accord; he scoffed, however, at the literary extremism and bohemian behavior of many of the young Romantics.

This was a period of great growth of the reading public in the nineteenth century, and in Spain as in other countries magazines began to flourish. These were eminently suitable vehicles for the short story and descriptive article about local customs. In fact, the addition of characters and the thread of a plot to a descriptive sketch transformed it into a rudimentary short story; and from these tales based on real life the short story evolved into the regional novel of Spain later in the century. This was the "Realism of Romanticism."

The many articles published in scattered issues of weekly magazines and other periodicals were gathered together and printed in the three volumes which are his best: *Panorama of Madrid* (1835), *Scenes of Madrid* (1842) and *Types and Characters* (1862). And in his seventies, Mesonero Romanos wrote a volume of nostalgic memoirs about the city as it was during his youth. It is to this day a valuable source work for the study of nineteenth-century Madrid from both the literary and historical viewpoints.

A large segment of his reading public consisted of young ladies of the middle and upper classes. This is often evident —as it is in the selection translated here—in the sentimental topics chosen as the basis for the author's gentle satire. The nearest equivalent of Mesonero Romanos in America is the Peruvian Ricardo Palma, who started to publish in the late nineteenth century his delightful "traditions" of old Lima.

The Short-Sighted Lover

"WHAT!" SOME CRITICAL reader will exclaim with surprise when he sees the title of this article. "Aren't even physical handicaps beyond the reach of *El Curioso's* barbs? Can it be that this fine fellow doesn't know it is not right for him to depart from the broad, general character of his sketches by dealing with such specific details? And who ever told him that it is proper to make fun of a physical handicap, at least unless it is accompanied by some moral defect?"

Patience, my friend. Let's straighten out this misunderstanding. It shouldn't be difficult; look at it this way. When certain physical defects are so common in a nation that they form part of its very make-up, can one who comments on their customs omit these defects and not utilize the opportunity to describe the many picturesque scenes they offer to him? If there were a nation composed of lame people, for example, would it not be interesting to learn about their military formations, their games, their dances and their calisthenics? Well, why not depict a lover who is short-sighted— when there is scarcely a lover who is not?

Moreover, who ever told you that this handicap—so fashionable nowadays—has not its moral aspects? Would it be too difficult to prove that its origin lies in today's lax customs, or in faulty upbringing, or in the extremism of youth? So you see, my friend, that this matter does fall quite naturally within the scope of my kindly criticism, and you will concede that it is not improper for me to speak of it—right? Well then, let us begin.

Many examples come to mind: all I need do is to select one. Today let us take up the case of Mauricio R . . . and may the lovely ladies who read these lines forgive me for choosing him to entertain them. And who is this fellow? He is, dear ladies, a young man twenty-three years old whose expressive features and sentimental air clearly reveal a tender heart readily inclined to fall in love. It should come as no surprise to you, therefore, that girls should find him charming. That is precisely what happened, and a few chance encounters on the streets and boulevards made him aware of his attractive appearance. Unfortunately, however, the young man has a major defect: he is near-sighted—very near-sighted—and this is going to handicap him in all his plans.

Just a moment, ladies; this is no laughing matter. Our hero certainly doesn't think so, nor does he take advantage of his defect (as many do) to be bolder and more demanding. He does not sport shiny gold-rimmed glasses on his nose, nor does he whip out an ever-present monocle to catch young ladies by surprise as they cast shy glances at him. Mauricio is romantic, but very considerate: he would rather deprive himself of pleasure than give displeasure to others. He might well have wished to wear eyeglassses all the time the way others do—without needing them—just to attract attention. But glasses are so awkward bobbing up and down to the rapid rhythm of the mazurka! For Mauricio, at twenty-three years of age, could not make up his

mind to stop dancing the mazurka. A good remedy, of
course, was the eyeglass he wore dangling by a ribbon; but in addition to the discreetness with which
he used it, how was he to guess what events were going
to happen so that he could be ready with it in his hand?
If some beautiful young lady were suddenly to turn
her lovely eyes toward him, or to drop her handkerchief
so he might have an opportunity to speak with her,
how could he foresee this a moment in advance? And
if, when he believed he was asking the prettiest girl in
the room to dance with him, he found himself saddled
with an Egyptian mummy, what good was the eyeglass
to him a moment later? Let's face it: his eyeglass was
no use to him at all, and Mauricio, who realized this,
was truly desperate.

Love, which for a long time had smitten him only
lightly, finally pierced his heart through and through.
One evening at a ball in the home of a certain *marquesa,*
Mauricio was dancing with Matilde de Láinez, and he
could not help revealing his feelings by a formal declaration of love. The girl, upon whom Mauricio's charms
no doubt had their effect, decided not to scold him

Faute d'avoir le temps de se mettre en courroux.[1]

And here we find our young man at love's most joyous
moment: the discovery that one's love is requited. By
now our young lovers had spoken at length; three
rigodons and one *galop* had simply fed the fires of their
passion. But the ball was ending, and the smitten
Mauricio renewed his declarations and pledges of love.
He took down the exact hour and minute that Matilde

[1] Because she had no time to become angry. (From one of La
Fontaine's *Fables.*) The interpolation of an untranslated line of
French poetry into the story indicates that the nineteenth-century
Spanish reading public was assumed to be familiar with the French
classics.

would appear on her balcony, the church where she
went to hear mass, the boulevards where she strolled
and met her friends, and the names of her mother's
favorite operas; in a word, all those little things that
you clever young fellows do not neglect in such cases.

But meantime the inexperienced Mauricio forgot to
make careful identification of Matilde's mother and an
elder sister, who were at the dance; he did not take note
of her father, a colonel in the cavalry; and, finally, he
did not dare to caution his beloved about his nearsighted-
ness. What happened later made him realize his mistake.

The next day, as soon as the appointed hour arrived,
he hurried to the street where his sweetheart lived.
He reviewed very carefully the information about her
house: Matilde had told him it was number 12, and
that it was on the corner of a certain street. But since
the house across the street, number 72, looked like
number 12 to the luckless lover, that was the one he
chose as the object of his siege.[2]

Matilde, who saw him arrive (girlish eyes, what you
cannot see when you are in love!), threw down her
sewing and hastened out to the balcony so her admirer
could see how lovely she looked in her daytime dress.
But it was all in vain, for Mauricio, who was only six
yards away on the other corner and whose eyes were
scanning the balconies of the house across the street,
paid scant attention to the beauty who had appeared on
the other balcony.

[2] Mesonero Romanos (whose initials, it will be noted, are the
same as Mauricio R . . .) is pointing out a defect in the system of
numbering the houses in Madrid. This was later changed so that
the even numbers would be on one side of the street and the odd
numbers on the other. An additional difficulty for the shortsighted
Mauricio was the European system (still in use) of writing the
numbers 7 and 1 in exactly the same way except for a little
horizontal line through the 7 to distinguish it from the 1.

Matilde's pride was piqued greatly by this unexpected slight. She coughed twice, and fluttered her handkerchief. All in vain. The heartsick lover glanced quickly at her, and then turned his back to busy himself with his appointed task. This went on for an hour or more, until the desperate young man, believing himself forgotten by his lady love, was strongly tempted to while away the time with the other girl who was sitting there so quietly. Finally he could resist no longer, and since otherwise he would be wasting the afternoon completely, he decided at last (although it broke his heart) to suspend his siege and talk to the haughty young lady across the way.

No sooner said than done. He crossed the street, marched straight beneath Matilde's balcony, and raised his head to speak to her. But at the same instant she hurled at his face the handkerchief she had been holding in her hand, and which she had tied into a mass of knots in her fury. Without saying a word to him, she swept inside and slammed the balcony windows. Mauricio untied the handkerchief and recognized the same embroidered initials he had seen on the one Matilde carried at the dance the night before. He peered closely at the house, and when he finally made out the number 12, how can we describe his desperation?

For three days and nights he walked up and down the street, to no avail. The balcony remained implacably closed, and the whole neighborhood—except the object of his affection—bore full witness to his sighs.

The third evening, one of her mother's favorite operas is being performed at the theater. From his orchestra seat he anxiously scans the auditorium with the aid of powerful opera glasses and sees nothing to attract him.

However, in one of the boxes he thinks he spies the girl's mother, accompanied by the cause of his suffering. He goes upstairs, walks through the corridors, and peers in at the entrance to the box . . . it is they, without a doubt. Mauricio virtually collapses making signs and grimaces, but without success. Finally the opera ends, and he waits for them to come downstairs. At the dimmest part of the staircase he goes over to the girl and says:

"Please forgive my mistake . . . if you come out on the balcony later I'll explain . . . meanwhile, here is your handkerchief."

"Sir! What are you saying?" a strange voice answered, as a flickering lamp (one of those lamps that light the stairways of our theaters so poorly) flared up and revealed to him that he was speaking to someone else, although she looked a lot like his beloved.

"Madame . . ."

"Why, this is my sister's handkerchief!"

"What's going on there, daughter?"

"Nothing, Mother; this gentleman is giving me one of Matilde's handkerchiefs."

"And how does this young man happen to have one of Matilde's handkerchiefs?"

"Madame . . . I . . . excuse me . . . the other day . . . the other night, I mean . . . at the *marquesa's* ball. . . ."

"That's right, Mother; this gentleman danced with sister, and it is not strange that she should have forgotten her handkerchief."

"Of course, that's right! She forgot it . . . forgot it. . . ."

"That's certainly strange. Well, sir, we thank you."

A bolt of lightning crashing at his feet could not have

upset Mauricio more. What distressed him most was the fact that in one corner of the handkerchief he had tied a note in which he spoke of his love, his declaration at the dance, and the mistake about the address; in short, it unfolded the whole tale—and he did not know what fate was in store for that piece of paper!

Trembling and hesitant, he followed the ladies at a distance until they went into their house and left him standing in the street in the deepest dejection. In vain he put his ear to the door to try to catch any loud talking; the voice of the night watchman calling twelve o'clock, and the noisy rattle of the sanitation trucks, were the only things that assailed his ears, and even his nostrils. Finally, tired of fruitless waiting, he went home and spent the whole night thinking about his unhappy love affair.

Meanwhile, what was happening inside the young lady's house? The mother, who had taken the handkerchief in order to scold the girl, discovered the note and read it. After the first flush of anger had passed, she decided (following the advice of the other sister) to say nothing, pretend ignorance, and write the suitor a brief note so curt that he would have no desire to come back. This they did, and the note, written in a woman's hand (all women's handwriting looks much the same) was signed and then sealed with wax, into which the girl's initials were pricked with a pin as additional identification. When this operation had been completed, they went to sleep, certain that the luckless lover would come to pace up and down in the street the next morning.

Indeed, no urging was needed, for eight o'clock had hardly struck when he was standing in a doorway across the street, not daring to look up. As he stood there he heard the balcony window open and—oh, joy!—a white hand threw down a bit of paper. The happy young man ran to catch it, and found that the balcony window had already been shut, and with it the hope in his heart.

It would be useless to try to describe the effect of that series of misfortunes upon Mauricio; suffice it to say that he renounced love *forever*. But he was young, after all, and two weeks later he felt otherwise. He went out to stroll along the Prado with a friend of his. It was one of those pleasant evenings in July that offer an invitation to enjoy the cool air beneath the leafy trees, so the two young men sat down and started to talk—of course —about their respective love affairs. Mauricio, with his inborn frankness, told his friend all about his recent adventures in minutest detail, right up to the heart-breaking dismissal that his unfortunate mistakes had brought upon him.

As he was finishing his account, he heard an abrupt movement on the bench close to his, where he observed seated among other people a military officer and a young lady. He leaned forward a bit, took out his eyeglass (why weren't you using it all along, you foolish fellow?) and discovered that the young lady seated right behind him, and who had heard the whole conversation, was none other than the lovely Matilde!

"How unkind of you!" was the only thing he could utter, while her father was busy calling over a boy to give him a light for his cigar.

"I didn't write that letter." (This reply he got after a quarter of an hour.)

"Well, who did?"

"I don't know. Bring it with you tonight; I'll be on the balcony at twelve o'clock."

Hope again poured its healing balm over the heart of

poor Mauricio. Full of flattering ideas, he awaited the appointed hour and raced to station himself beneath her balcony.

Yes, there she is. Now he sees a pair of eyes shining brightly, now he makes out a white hand, and now . . . But, oh how well Shakespeare puts it when he says that

> *When sorrows come, they come not single spies,*
> *But in battalions.*[3]

That night her father had felt like taking a breath of fresh air after dinner, and it was he who was leaning upon the balcony railing—much to the dismay of Matilde, who kept urging him to get to bed in order to avoid the dampness.

"My darling," said Mauricio in honeyed tones, "is that you?"

"Matilde," the father said softly to the girl, "does this have anything to do with you?"

"With me, father? No, sir; I don't know. . . ."

"No? Well, this must have something to do with you or with your sister."

"Just so you may see whether I had cause for being angry," continued the devoted suitor, "here comes the note. . . ."

"Let's see, now, daughter. Inside, inside! Bring me a light; I'm going to read this. . . ."

Suiting the action to the word, he goes in to the parlor, glaring at his daughter with menacing eyes. He opens the note and reads:

"*Sir: If at the marquesa's ball that night my indiscretion caused you to hope wildly that. . . .*"

[3] Unlike the French verse from La Fontaine, the English is translated into Spanish by Mesonero Romanos for the benefit of his readers. (The quotation is from Act IV, Scene 5, of *Hamlet.*)

"Heavens! What is this I see? My wife's hand-writing!"

"Oh, father!"

"Shameful woman! To go around at forty years of age raising wild hopes!"

"But, father. . . ."

"Just watch me wake her up and raise the roof!"

And indeed, he did just that. For more than an hour the shouting and wailing and weeping disturbed the entire neighborhood and greatly frightened the "phantom lover," who could catch from the street only part of the unrestrained exchange of words.

His warm heart and his honor would not permit him to let everyone suffer any longer on his account. He knocked resolutely at the front door, and when the father came out on the balcony said to him:

"Sir, please be kind enough to listen to a word of explanation of my conduct."

The father seized two pistols, hurried downstairs, and opened the door.

"Choose one!" he said.

"Please calm yourself, sir," the young man answered. "I am a gentleman, and my name is ——. My family is well known. An unfortunate misunderstanding has caused me to upset the peace of your household. I simply cannot see this happen without explaining the circumstances to you."

Here he made a detailed and frank explanation of all the facts; the mother and the daughters confirmed them, and with this the jealous colonel calmed down. The next day at Matilde's house the *marquesa* formally introduced Mauricio, and the father, informed of his background, offered no opposition.

From then on this love story continued in a calmer

vein. Those who like to follow such matters to their conclusion will be happy to learn that Mauricio and his sweetheart were married, in spite of the fact that she did not seem so beautiful to him when he looked at her in a strong light and with eyeglasses, because her face was pockmarked and she had other slight defects. However, she had many excellent virtues, and Mauricio disregarded her physical endowments. All he had to do, in order to forget them, was to perform one simple operation, which was . . . to take off his glasses!

Ramón Gómez de la Serna (1891–   )

. . . is an incredibly prolific author who has written a young library—well over a hundred books. Born in Madrid, like Larra and Mesonero Romanos, he adores his native city, particularly Old Madrid. He has written a splendid biography of Goya (his favorite artist), and critical works on El Greco, Azorín and Valle-Inclán. He is also a dramatist, and a novelist of note. But it is in the field of humor—a wry, sardonic humor—that he excels. His roots go far back into Spanish satire—back through Goya's etchings to Quevedo's *Dreams* and Góngora's baroque concepts. Around him, particularly in the Café Pombo in Madrid, there grew up a whole cult called *"Ramonismo"* which had considerable influence on his contemporaries during the period after World War I, when many "isms" were flourishing—cubism, dadaism, futurism and others. The story here translated is typical of Gómez de la Serna's tongue-in-cheek imagination in this medium.

His greatest "invention" is the *greguería*, a kind of pixie thought that flashes through his mind and is expressed in an epigram or aphorism. Ramón, as he is called, has written hundreds of thousands of them. He himself defines a *greguería* as a confused clamoring and says that "in old dictionaries it meant the cries of little pigs running after their mother." The analogy with the confused, squealing state of modern society is sardonic. Here are a few samples of these absurd random thoughts he expresses so pungently:

"A rainbow is the ribbon that Nature puts on after washing her hair."

"Seagulls were born from the handkerchiefs that wave good-bye in harbors."

"Zeros are the eggs from which all the other numbers were hatched."

"Thunder: a trunk falling down the stairway of heaven."

"When a woman orders fruit salad for two, she is compounding the original sin."

"When a star falls, there is a run in the stocking of Night."

"Can it be that the secret of high tides is that somewhere, at a given time, God is bathing in the sea?"

"Penguins are babies that have left the table with their bibs on."

In his personal eccentricities Ramón has become a living legend. He has delivered lectures from a trapeze, and from an elephant's back; he has had a regular street-lamp installed in his room; he carries in his breast pocket several red-ink fountain pens which, he says, are constantly being refilled from his heart; and his unconventional, madcap behavior is a byword in Madrid. The following short story is a typical "Ramonism."

The Triangular House

WHEN ADOLFO SUREDA decided to marry, he resolved to carry out a promise he had made to himself: to live in a house built especially for him according to plans that were entirely unique. It would be a house with exceptional architecture so that he and his wife could look forward to an exceptional married life free from the usual petty annoyances.

Adolfo sought out the recent School of Architecture graduate who had been the most daring in the plans he drew for his final examinations—those marvelous pieces of rubbish usually thrown out afterward by the school. The young man's name was Nicasio García Alijo, and he accepted the commission with determination.

"It will be something never seen before," he promised.

"But," Adolfo advised him, "don't let yourself be carried away by Yugoslavian architecture."

The young architect began to draw up the plans immediately, rejecting all those Basque cottages that are so common: somber, weather-beaten, aloof, and austerely sealed against the rains. Neither did he wish the house to be original because of its decorative appeal; and none of those picture windows set in a severely simple structure, or classic doorways, or the projecting overhang of frowning eaves. The uniqueness of the house had to be in its soaring outlines and its novel character.

His pencil moved across the paper in a reverie; it was as if he were doodling again in the margin of a schoolbook. The swirls of the pencil kept covering up his sketches, and with the smudgy end of the eraser he had just rubbed out those designs that revolted him, when finally, in a hidden corner of his imagination, he found a type of house that pleased him. The owner would have a house that stood out among all those standardized little dwellings that dot the countryside like decorated boxes. He turned the paper over and put the thumbtacks into new holes. Then he took the drawing triangle and whit-whit-whit he traced an isosceles triangle:

Next he planned the front windows: a bull's-eye opening high up in the garret, two triangular windows for the servants' quarters on the third floor, and three triangular windows on the second floor. The doorway was another isosceles triangle.

He went ahead carefully with his plans, overcoming all difficulties with his ingenuity. The two sloping concrete sides would eliminate the need for a roof, since the rain would run down the smooth surface. And he would place a kind of reinforced cowl over each window so the water would run down on either side of it.

Adolfo Sureda was enchanted with the plans for the house. Surveying was started on a piece of land he owned in El Sotillo, which was an open area on the outskirts of town just before the real countryside began. When the digging struck solid rock they began the construction of the foundation, that gaunt, planned ruin which is the first part exposed to the weather and the last to remain when a windstorm sweeps away what has been built above it.

2

The house was almost ready. The acute triangle was now a bold, proud fact: it had personality, and it had sacrificed everything to an ideal. A lightning rod was added, although the architect declared that none was needed because the lightning, finding nothing to strike when it came in contact with the sides of the building, would simply slide down the toboggan-like slopes.

Unconventional furniture was bought, and some pieces—the dining room table and the hatrack—were made to order in triangular shape to harmonize with the house.

Opinions about the house varied widely: those who wished to avoid argument limited themselves to saying, "My dear! What rare taste!"

The ultra-conservative: "I wouldn't live in a house like that if they gave it to me!"

The impressionable young lady: "To me it would seem like living under an open staircase."

The man hypersensitive to pain: "It looks as though

you must go around bumping your head everywhere."

A friend of the family: "One of its advantages is that if anyone sends you a message it won't get lost."

Girl friends of the bride-to-be: "I don't know how you can marry such an eccentric!"

A fanciful friend: "From a distance it looks like a piece of a house that has been in a knife fight!"

In the neighborhood, people began to call it "the melon slice."

And so the solemn wedding day arrived, and the newlyweds took possession of their triangular home, which they entered as if it were a fun house at the fair. They were followed by the girl's mother, a maiden aunt, and the unhappy father, upon whom the idea was beginning to dawn that leaving his daughter in such a house was like launching her on a theatrical career.

When the time came to say good-bye, the mother began to cry, and said between sobs:

"My darling daughter! How it grieves me to leave you in a house like this!"

Finally, the maiden aunt straightened out the lace on the bed covering, and, after kissing Remedios and shaking Adolfo's hand in Masonic style, she pulled the parents toward the street door. They all went out, bending low as they passed through the broad triangular doorway.

3

The triangular house saw very happy—if somewhat childish—days: play-filled mornings in which Adolfo and Remedios seemed to return to the early innocence of games with construction sets, when they evolved gay structures out of sad, cubist blocks.

"Misfortune," they both thought, "cannot possibly come into a toy house whose doorway is so different from the ones She usually seeks out."

The beseeching eyes of the triangular windows, raised toward Heaven, pleaded mystically for happiness.

But the house that had revealed such childish innocence during those first months of its occupation entered the regular ranks of mundane houses that grow weather-beaten and learn all about ordinary life beneath the sun.

"Now," the boulevard in Sotillo seemed to say to it, "you are just one more house in the neighborhood and you are on your own."

That same day, there appeared next to its door the first marks made by boys who steal charcoal sticks at the coal dealer's for just that purpose. The door knocker also sounded three times, lifted by some unknown prankster's hand, and a few days later the vestibule door was found nailed tight to its frame.

The mailman began to bring letters addressed to "Mr. Triangle-House Owner," in which the most absurd things were said and the most frightful threats were made.

The mysterious "Order of the Fiery Triangle" made him its honorary president and expected him to acquiesce completely: its meetings would henceforth be held in the shadow of his house, but he should not consider himself invited because he was only honorary president. And indeed, within a few days he noticed a great gathering behind the house and suspected that it must be the meeting of the "Fiery Triangle," although he was less sure of this when he saw that they were dividing up the contents of a wallet.

"Who wants the identification card? It may be useful to somebody when he wants to assume a false name some time."

"Pass it over," said a man who was covered with soot like a coal man.

"Who wants a little packet of calling cards that go with the wallet?"

In view of that nightly auction, as it were, Adolfo had iron bars put across the lower windows, thus crucifying the triangles.

Faced with all these developments, he began to wonder about the responsibility he had taken on when he moved into the triangular house. Its triangular façade was the most tempting target for blows from unexpected quarters. He did not wish to exchange impressions with his wife, but it worried him to think that his house was the center for the cult of triangularism.

4

The triangular house was happy: it was going to see sons who would defend it from outsiders who might convert it into a quadrangular house by some cheap alterations.

Remedios was expecting a child. Everything in the triangular house was topsy-turvy, and the neighbors who knew about the coming event looked at the house as if it were unworthy of a serious thing like the birth of a child.

Their son was about to be born in the playhouse. Until that time everyone had been passing through the difficult period that precedes the opening performance of a play—those moments in which every comedy seems as though it will turn out to be a tragedy.

The expensive doctor who gives injections so that

the child will not be brought forth in sorrow, as it is decreed, was polishing and sterilizing a big basin and was ripping open packages of cotton and helping himself to gauze as if he were the proprietor of his own drugstore. Everything was ready for the ringing of the bell at the moment of birth.

"It will take place at five minutes to twelve," the doctor had said, and he was famous for never making a mistake about the time of birth because he carried a watch he had bought in Germany just for these cases. And indeed the blessed event did take place at five minutes to twelve; one after another, three sons were born.

The father's astonishment was enormous, and along with it other problems began to arise: for example, his friends were going to look upon him as some kind of freak, and in addition he was suddenly being made to seem a much older man than he really was, because he now had three children.

Only in mid-afternoon, when all his tenseness had subsided, did it occur to him that the triangular house might have been the cause of this joke, which was much more serious than those that had gone before. Ideas like that come to people who are connoisseurs of the extraordinary.

"Now," he thought finally, facing the consequences, "the three angles of the triangle have been found, and these boys should be given names to fit with the letters A B C which label the triangle. Therefore the first-born will be named Augusto, the second Benito, and the third César."

People in the neighborhood smiled when they spoke of the incident:

"You can keep your triangular houses!"

"And even more outlandish things are bound to happen to him!"

"Poor boys! What an unpleasant life awaits them!"

5

The three children grew up alike, and were happy to live in the house that all their little playmates knew as the triangle house. At school they were asked rude questions:

"Is it true that everything you eat is served in the shape of a pyramid?"

"Is it true that you have a cook with three arms?"

"Is it true that your father plays the three-holed flute very well?"

"Does your mother walk sideface, like an Egyptian on a mural?"

Every day they would come home to their father with questions like that, which deeply disturbed him. Adolfo kept asking himself more and more insistently whether he had made a sizeable mistake in having the triangular house built.

Benito had a pronounced tendency toward a sharp-pointed head, and in the other two boys it was becoming noticeable, too.

There was much unrest in the triangular household, and many servant girls had to be let go because they could not work in a house which looked like that— "the house everyone feels he must say something about." With the children's nurses there had already been similar difficulties because they stated flatly that they could not sleep beneath that roof which seemed to press down on them.

One afternoon as Adolfo was returning home, drawn

by the warm comfort of its walls—troublesome but beloved—he noticed that a gentleman was grimacing in
front of his windows. Adolfo stopped, and took cover
behind a clump of trees. The gentleman had a scraggly
beard which he was tugging at nervously. Then, as if
Remedios were late in coming to the window or in
making some prearranged signal, he took out a piece
of paper and began to write on it.

Adolfo advanced upon the unknown man, and asked
him angrily what he meant by looking at his house
like that.

"Sir, I am a mathematician—a geometer—and your
house intrigues me because it poses new problems in
geometry and trigonometry. Here are the data for the
problem . . ."

And the geometer showed Adolfo the paper with his
figures:

Calculation of Angle A

$$\tan \tfrac{1}{2} A = \sqrt{\frac{(p-b)(p-c)}{p(p-a)}}$$

Adolfo breathed a sigh of relief, and invited the
geometer to come in and rest for a while. With visible
emotion the geometer then said:

"Oh! How happy you make me, sir, letting me go
into your triangular dwelling! I would never even have
dreamed of this . . . I shall see the problem from the
inside!"

Adolfo and the geometer walked through the triangular doorway and went into Adolfo's study.

"Could we first go up to the attic? That is where
the apex of the triangle is formed."

"By all means . . . right away."

The geometer made some notations, and then asked to go down to the rooms on either side of the doorway, where the two base angles were formed. They went down, and the geometer, as if he were a second architect, measured the house with a long measuring tape which he curled up again as if he were winding a pocket music-box.

"Now I shall be happy to rest in your fine study," he said at last, after taking more notes. Together they went up to the first floor, and once inside the study he exclaimed with surprise:

"Ah! Your desk is triangular, too! How marvelous!"

There was a pause, which was broken by the geometer, who said:

"You must be very happy in this house, in which the hearth is thrice blessed."

"That is not quite so . . . I am somewhat uneasy . . . Strange things are happening around here . . . Fate plays cruel tricks upon me. Not long ago, some prankster put an advertisement in the newspapers saying that I needed a secretary, and the whole town paraded through here. My house is also the meeting place for sweethearts on Sundays: they find it so easy to make a date 'opposite the triangular house.' My whole life is getting complicated because I live in this triangulated house, which is what I prefer to call it."

"This is happening to you," the mathematician replied, "because you are not a geometer. If you grasped the triangular sense of the house you would be invincible: there is nothing more devoid of problems—or more clean-cut in its arrangement of space—than a triangle. Would you like me to instruct you in these matters? It has been my lifelong study. All we need by way of equipment is a blackboard."

"I'm ready . . . We'll start the lessons tomorrow
. . . I'll expect you between six and seven o'clock."

And Adolfo said good-bye to the geometer with the
deference that an adult student shows toward his professor of English.

6

Adolfo specialized in triangles, and grew steadily
more confident about his triangular house. He was
amazed at how the triangle kept being solved, thanks to
equations and calculations. There were no corners or
wasted spaces in his house; logically, it was superior to
all other houses. He and the geometer had even decided
to collaborate in writing an essay on "The Triangle: A
Study in Depth, or, The Intimate Exegesis of the Living
Triangle."

Remedios, in the face of those speculations by the
geometer and her husband, was growing bored—
triangularly. She would bring in their coffee as a brain
stimulant and would leave the room scarcely noticed,
for they would reach out blindly for the handles of
their cups and drain them at a single gulp.

The touch of Adolfo's hands, gritty from handling
chalk all afternoon, had become repulsive to Remedios,
and she was weary of his way of amusing himself by
looking at three points of the compass and calling his
sons by their initials ("Come over here, A; come over
here, B; come over here, C") so he could touch their
slightly pointed heads for a moment. And at bedtime
Adolfo felt the deep kind of weariness from abstract
thinking that makes a man turn his back to his wife.

The all-absorbing lessons in descriptive geometry continued every afternoon just as usual, until one day
Adolfo received an anonymous letter in which he was
informed that his wife was deceiving him while he was

theorizing at the blackboard. After greeting the geometer, who removed his top hat as if it were a wig, Adolfo led him with an air of mystery into one corner of the study and showed him the note.

"Ah!" exclaimed the geometer. "This must be studied as one more problem: the domestic triangle. I had hoped that it might not happen—but it had to happen . . . and better now than later, after all."

"Great heavens! Better that it had never happened!" Adolfo answered.

The geometer went to the blackboard and rubbed out what was written there with the decisive movements of a fireman putting out a blaze. Then he set about solving the problem.

"You form a scalene triangle . . . we deduce this, not only because of your unequal qualities but also because the moment your wife—angle A—found someone attuned to her nature, you were the perpendicular angle, angle B. Now, since we know angles A and B, all we need do is to find angle C. The problem is extremely simple because A is, of course, equal to C, which is the unknown . . . Does some Cousin of your wife's have free access to the house?"

"Yes. Enrique."

"Well, that's the man."

"Is the proof positive?"

"Geometrically! Q.E.D."

Adolfo went out of the study, found his wife, and accused her:

"So! It's Enrique, isn't it?"

"How did you know?"

"Trigonometric formulas never fail."

"Ah!" she finally exclaimed, giving herself away.

That same evening the triangular house was left

unoccupied. Adolfo went to live in a boarding house, and Remedios went home to her parents with the three boys.

The following day there appeared on the front of the isosceles dwelling a triangular sign which read:

Fernán Caballero (1796–1877)

. . . was the masculine pen name taken by Cecilia Böhl de Faber, daughter of the learned German consul in Seville. Her mother, Doña Francisca Larrea, came from an old Andalusian family. Her father, with his research into Spanish poetry and drama, and his translation into Spanish of German works of literary criticism, was one of the important forerunners of the Romantic movement in Spain. Cecilia was born while the family was in Switzerland, and she also attended schools abroad. Despite her international background and education, she considered herself "very Andalusian." She spent almost her whole life in southern Spain, where she devoted herself to gathering legends, folklore, tales and stories of the people of her region. She died in Seville.

Her first novel, too, was very Andalusian—the tragic tale of *La Gaviota* (*The Seagull*), a singer who forsook her German husband, a doctor, for a bullfighter. Published in 1849, this work was full of regionalism, customs and real-life situations; as such, it initiated the great outpouring of regional-realist novels in Spain during the rest of the nineteenth century.

Other novels followed, all with the same moralizing note. Fernán Caballero believed that the novelist should strive not only to entertain but also to uplift. A deeply religious woman, she does not flinch from depicting reality, even in its most sordid and anti-social details, but always with the pious purpose of pointing a moral. For example, in *The Family of Alvareda* (1856) she depicts adultery, murder and banditry, but the killer—though a pitiful figure—pays on the gallows for his weakness and crimes.

One of the chief themes in her novels is the corruption of the city—Seville, in her novel *Clemencia* (1862)—and the peace and virtue to be found in the country among simple, religious folk. This note was to be sounded again and again by virtually all the regional novelists who followed Fernán Caballero during the later nineteenth century.

In addition to her work as a novelist, Doña Cecilia wrote many novelettes, short stories and articles describing regional customs. Among her Andalusian stories is the one translated here. It is based on real life: the eighteenth-century soldier-poet José Cadalso was killed at the siege of Gibraltar under similar circumstances in 1782, while Spanish forces were pinning down some of the British power during the American Revolution when France and Spain were helping the budding United States.

The Two Friends

THE SUN BEAT DOWN in burning rays upon a dry and barren Andalusian plain. No water flowed through its streams or brooks, and the flowers and young spring plants lay wilted; the only green things were some thorn bushes, mastic trees and cactus, whose harshness resists the rigors of the seasons. Clouds of dust were being blown by a brisk breeze from the east, hot as the breath of a volcano. The blue sky and bright sunshine seemed to mock the tortured earth. Only the cattle of the region, with their resistant hides, and the spirited Spaniard, with his stoic scorn of all physical suffering, were able to endure that fiery blast—they by sleeping and he by singing!

There could be seen on this plain on the twentieth of August of 1782 the signs of a recent battle: dead horses, broken weapons, plants trampled down and covered with blood. In the distance a British detachment was marching off in good order; nearby, the commander of a Spanish cavalry unit was busy regrouping his impatient soldiers and spirited horses in order to pursue the English who, though fewer in number, were withdrawing with the calm of victors.

In the field where the battle had taken place, a

young man was seated on a rock at the foot of an olive tree, with his pale face resting against its trunk; another young man, whose face revealed deep desperation, was kneeling at his feet and trying with his handkerchief to staunch the flow of his friend's blood, which was pouring from a great gash in his chest.

"Ah, Felix, Felix!" he exclaimed with profound anguish. "You are going to die, and all on account of me! Your brave breast took the blow that was destined for me. Why, my devoted friend, did you save me from a glorious death and leave me a life of despair and grief?"

"Don't despair, Ramiro," his friend said in a soft voice. "I am weak because I have lost a lot of blood, but my wound is not a fatal one. Meanwhile, Ramiro, don't you see that your own hand, that quickly avenged me, is wounded, too?"

"Aid," said Ramiro without listening to him, "only prompt aid might be able to save you! But left all alone as we are, how can I get it for you? I cannot bring myself to leave you; at least we shall die together, Felix!"

At this moment they heard the gallop of a horse. Ramiro, gripped by anxiety, turned his eyes toward the source of the sound and spied their faithful orderly who, separated from them during the fight and deeply concerned for their safety, was looking for them.

Felix de Arahal and Ramiro de Lérida belonged to two families that had been united by bonds of deep friendship for a long time. Brought up together, they had been attached to the royal household and were now serving in the same regiment, where they had risen at an early age to the rank of captain.

Felix, somewhat older than Ramiro, and with a stronger character, greater maturity of judgment and a more even temperament, had a certain ascendancy over his friend. This, instead of diminishing the fine quality of their friendship, added to that feeling: in one, the consideration and gratitude that inspire the protection that is received, and in the other the interest and attachment that engender the protection that is given. After so evident a proof of devotion as that which Felix had just shown Ramiro by facing death to save the latter's life, which he had risked so imprudently, Ramiro's strong affection for his friend was now boundless. He looked upon Felix as his guardian angel and, extremist that he was, he would have exhausted his strength and health in helping his friend during the long illness caused by the wound, had not Felix himself prevented it by exercising the prerogatives of his friendship and his weakened condition.

*

Through the streets of San Roque, where they were stationed during the siege of Gibraltar, the Princess Regiment was on parade, preceded by a military band that was playing with wild abandon. Lovely ladies had come out on their balconies to see the soldiers who were greeting them with their lively music and their flattering glances.

"Look up there and you'll see what I call a beautiful woman!" said Ramiro to Felix, who was marching at his side.

Felix, still pale, raised his head and saw on the balcony of one of the finest houses in the city a young lady of striking beauty, half hidden behind the profusion of flower pots on her balcony, like an hour of joy preceded by hours of hope.

"You certainly are one to ferret out pretty girls," answered Felix, smiling.

They went by. From time to time Ramiro would turn his head to look again at that girl who had attracted his attention so much. She in turn followed the two officers with her glances: one of them tall, pale, and of erect and aristocratic bearing; the other, shorter but agile, well-built, haughty and high-spirited.

*

"It wasn't very brilliant, but at least we can say that the ball last night was quite gay," Ramiro was saying to a group of officers who were gathered in the city's main square.

"It must have seemed that way to you," said a lieutenant of cavalry, who was just as indefatigable in reconnoitering in the ballroom as on the battlefield, "because you certainly enjoyed yourself there."

"But enough of jokes, gentlemen," replied Ramiro. "Unfortunately, the siege of the fortress, which drags on so slowly, keeps us all idle, and that is what causes this foolish gossip."

"I can see that you're all wrapped up in some intrigue," Felix said to his friend when they left the others, "because you have grown so serious. Don't forget the old couplet, Ramiro:

I fell in love 'neath her balcony sighing:
I began by laughing and ended crying."

"Just introspection and rationalization!" Ramiro answered. "Look at those fortifications, Felix, spewing death upon us. God only knows how many hours we have left to live! Besides, ask old folks how long their first twenty-five years lasted. Let's enjoy life, Felix, while we can!"

*

Poor Ramiro found no enjoyment, however, when he rose from his bed without having slept all night. Leaning upon the railing of his balcony, he blinked and hardly looked at the sun which was rising over the horizon, rousing the world like a luminous bell. With his fiery temperament, Ramiro's love had reached the point of desperation due to the insuperable obstacles that were placed in his path. Quiet, timid meetings in church, a few words through the barred window at night when he could come in disguise, and pitiful notes that contained tears rather than words, were all he had to keep his supreme passion alive—a youthful, exuberant, Andalusian passion, yearning for a future and without a past to sustain it by memories. Ramiro cursed the countless obstacles, and surrendered to deep despair.

He was so absorbed in his sad thoughts that it was necessary for María, the good old woman who was Laura's nurse and confidante, to cough twice as she passed beneath his window before he noticed her. Ramiro hurried down and followed the kind woman at a distance, not daring to look at anyone for fear of being recognized.

After many turns María reached a deserted street on one side of which rose the high, straight walls of a convent and on the other the Magistrate's garden wall. María stopped here. Ramiro came up, and she handed him a note which he opened hurriedly. It contained these few words: "I am free this evening and can see you."

Who, without Ramiro's impassioned heart and burning love, can appreciate his ecstasy? Fervently he kissed the note, which this time was not stained by tears but showed by its trembling, poorly-formed letters the haste with which it had been written. With the same fervor he kissed María's bony hands. Then he took out a well-filled purse and handed it to her, calling her his guardian angel, his loving mother, his kind friend. But María's face suddenly changed its expression; she straightened her bent body, her lusterless eyes flashed fire, and she looked at Ramiro from head to foot with indignant pride.

"Señor," she said, "just who do you think I am? What I have done for love of my little girl may be weakness, but to do it for money would be infamy!"

And she disappeared through the garden gate.

Felix, when he came into his friend's room to have breakfast, was shocked to find him plunged into a fit of the wildest desperation. Storming and raging, he was pulling out locks of his handsome, curly hair, and was hurling anything he could get his hands upon . . . He was smashing the furniture!

"What's the matter with you, Ramiro?" Felix asked.

His only reply was:

"Curse this military career! Curse this gilded servitude! Curse the Colonel, an absolute tyrant! Curse the day I received these epaulets, and with them a chain impossible to break!"

"But my dear fellow," Felix said to him, "I simply cannot understand why you are so upset. Have you had some difficulty with the Colonel?"

"Ah! It's not a question of difficulty; it's my whole life's happiness, that's all! I have no secrets from you. Here . . . read this!"

He handed Laura's note to Felix, who, after reading it, said:

"Well, what about it?"

"What about it!" Ramiro replied. "Am I not the most unfortunate man alive?"

"These lines," answered Felix, "give me exactly the opposite impression."

"But don't you know my name is on the duty roster to command the outpost tonight?" exclaimed Ramiro.

"And is that the reason for your despair?" said Felix. "That is what they call making a mountain out of a molehill. I'll go on duty for you, and you can take my place when it's my turn."

Ramiro clasped his friend in his arms and said:

"Felix . . . Felix, my dear fellow . . . you were born just to make me happy; you are my salvation; you are a benevolent being who strews flowers upon my life's path. How can I ever repay your tender, generous friendship?"

"But have I done anything," Felix replied, "that you would not have done in my place, my dear Ramiro?"

The latter made no reply, but pressed his friend to his heart, which was as full of affection and friendship as it was of hope and gratitude.

*

The sun was rising over the horizon in all its monotonous majesty. How happy Ramiro was! His whole being seemed to overflow with pride, gratitude and tenderness. He cherished in the innermost depths of his heart all the emotions called forth by a truly requited love. Intoxicated with happiness, he blessed his lot. In his ecstasy he did not notice a cavalry lieutenant who was coming up to greet him. Ramiro finally saw him and started to cross the street, making believe he was preoccupied. But the lieutenant hastened over to him and said:

"How glad I am to see you, Lérida! I thought you were on duty at the outpost!"

"Well, what about it?"

"A nasty bit of business," the cavalryman replied. "The British made an attack, and the commander of the outpost was killed."

*

One Sunday in the year 1833, many lovely ladies wearing flowers, ribbons and white mantillas, and many elegant young men on foot and on horseback, were hurrying toward the promenade. The happy throng was streaming toward the left, while toward the right a noteworthy contrast could be seen. A Capuchin monk, standing on an embankment, was preaching to a great crowd of people who formed a fan-like semicircle about him. A short distance away, an Englishman seated beneath a tree was drawing in his sketch-book the venerable face of the Capuchin. A peasant who was looking over the Englishman's shoulder smiled and said with the frank cordiality of a Spaniard, for whom a glance serves as an introduction:

"Upon my life, it's the spit and image of him! You are a great painter, señor, and if you are English, as I believe, you are probably unaware that that peaceful, saintly man may have killed some of your forebears."

The Englishman looked at the Spaniard with surprise, and the latter continued:

"Yes, señor, his sword was brave and mighty back in

1782. He distinguished himself at the siege of Gibraltar, until . . . But it's a long story."

The Englishman begged him to tell it, and the good man—who wanted nothing else—recounted the tale you have just read. And the Spaniard said in conclusion:

"Seeing so clearly the hand of God, who punished him with such a frightful calamity, and beside himself with grief for having caused the death of his friend, Ramiro saw only two alternatives: to die, or to do penance. Thank God he was a good Christian, and had sufficient courage to choose the latter!"

The Englishman looked at the monk with renewed interest. He now possessed the microscope, we might say, with which he could see beneath that humble, quiet exterior. But in vain did he seek on that old face any trace of tears, a tinge of grief or a look of sad remembrance. All had disappeared from that calm and venerable countenance. And this complete change was not the work of time: a lofty virtue had freed his heart from this world and raised it to those heights in which, as the eloquent poet Lamartine puts it,

Even the memory faded away, leaving not a trace.

Pedro Antonio de Alarcón (1833–1891)

. . . is best known internationally for his short novel *The Three-Cornered Hat* (1874), which, when made into a ballet in 1919, was set to music by Manuel de Falla. In Spain Alarcón is still one of the most widely read of its great nineteenth-century writers, not only for this sparkling literary gem but also for his many other novels and especially for his delightful Andalusian short stories.

Alarcón was born in the province of Granada. His family, a distinguished one, was impoverished by the War of Independence (1808–1814), and could not afford to let young Pedro complete his law degree at the University of Granada. He transferred to Theology, but this was not to his liking and he left the university to become a crusading journalist. A fiery young Liberal, he dipped his pen in vitriol and attacked the regime of the inept Queen Isabella II, and the excessive influence of the Church and the Army. Challenged to a duel, he owed his life to the gallantry of his adversary, who fired into the air.

A change of heart came over Alarcón, and he enlisted as a private to fight in the war Spain was waging in North Africa (1859–1860). He was wounded in action, and twice decorated. His brilliant coverage of the campaign for a Madrid daily, published later in book form, won him fame and funds to continue his literary career. Upon his return to Spain he was elected to Parliament as a Conservative; he espoused the Catholic cause and the constitutional monarchy of Alfonso XII. After the publication of *The Three-Cornered Hat* he gave up politics and devoted himself to letters. He was elected to the Royal Spanish Academy.

By the time of Alarcón's death in 1891, his writings totalled twenty volumes in such diverse fields as poetry, geographical-historical studies, essays, drama, novels, memoirs, and short stories. His "thesis" novels all supported religion, morality, and the Conservative viewpoint during the Spanish political storms of the nineteenth century. Although rather heavy with moralizing, they were best sellers in their day.

Alarcón's best works, however, are his novelettes and short stories, rich in Andalusian color, lore and legend. The selection translated here, still a great favorite with Spanish readers, appeared in his collection called *National Tales*, published in 1881.

The Gypsy Fortune

IN AUGUST of 1816—I am not sure of just which day it was—there came to the door of the headquarters of the Captain General in Granada a certain ragged, unsightly gypsy some sixty years of age. A sheep-shearer by occupation and Heredia by name, he was mounted on a scrawny, broken-down, black burro whose harness consisted of just a rope tied round its neck. As soon as he had dismounted he announced quite coolly that he wished to see the Captain General.

Needless to say, such presumption aroused in turn the resistance of the sentinel, the laughter of the orderlies, and the doubts and hesitation of the aides-de-camp before it came to the attention of His Excellency Don Eugenio Portocarrero, Count of Montijo, at that time Captain General of the former Kingdom of Granada. But as that dignitary was a man of kindly disposition and had heard a great deal about Heredia, who was notorious for his tricks and his love of shady deals involving other people's property (always with the permission of the duped owner), he ordered them to let the gypsy pass. The latter came into His Excellency's office taking two steps forward and one backward, which was the way he walked in such serious situations. Falling to his knees he exclaimed:

"Praised be Most Holy Mary! And long life to Your Excellency, master of our whole little world!"

"Get up! Stop your flattery and tell me what this is all about," replied the Count with seeming severity.

Heredia, too, put on a serious expression, and said with cool effrontery, "Well, sir, I have come to collect my thousand *reales*."

"What thousand *reales*?"

"Those offered by proclamation a few days ago to anyone bringing in information about Parrón."

"Indeed! You knew him?"

"No, sir."

"Then. . . ."

"But I know him now."

"What!"

"It is very simple. I looked for him; I saw him; I bring the information, and now I want my reward."

"Are you sure you have seen him?" exclaimed the Captain General with an interest that overcame his doubts.

The gypsy burst out laughing and answered, "I see! Your Excellency is probably thinking: 'This gypsy is just like all of them, and wants to deceive me.' May God never forgive me if I am lying! Yesterday I saw Parrón."

"But do you realize the importance of what you are saying? Do you know that for the past three years we have been hunting for that monster, that bloodthirsty bandit nobody knows or has ever been able to see? Do you know that every day in different parts of these mountains he robs travellers and then kills them in cold blood, saying that dead men tell no tales, and that that is the only reason the law never catches up with him? In short, do you know that to see Parrón means death?"

The gypsy laughed and said, "And doesn't Your Excellency know that what a gypsy cannot do, no one on earth is able to do? Doesn't anyone know when our laughter—or our weeping—is genuine? Does Your Excellency know any fox as sly as we are? I repeat, General: not only have I seen Parrón, but I have talked with him!"

"Where?"

"On the road to Tozar."

"Give me proof."

"You shall hear, Your Excellency. A week ago yesterday morning my little burro and I fell into the hands of robbers. They tied my hands tight and led me through some sort of devil's gorge until they came to a clearing where the bandits had their camp. A cruel suspicion made me sick at heart: 'Can these be Parrón's men?' I kept saying to myself. 'If so, there is no hope. They will kill me, because that accursed wretch has decreed that eyes that see his face shall never see another thing.'

"I was absorbed in these thoughts when I found myself in the presence of a man dressed in a flashy and expensive Andalusian costume. He tapped me on the shoulder, and in a charming manner said: 'My friend, I am Parrón.'

"Hearing this, I fell backward instantly. The bandit burst out laughing, and I rose, badly shaken. Kneeling down, I exclaimed in every tone of voice I could contrive: 'May your soul be blessed, oh king of men! Who would not recognize you by that princely bearing God gave you? May there be a mother to bear more sons like you! Let me embrace you, my boy. May this old gypsy die a miserable death if he wasn't longing to meet you and tell your fortune, and to kiss that lordly hand of yours! Consider me at your service. Do you want me to show you how to trade dead donkeys for live ones? Do you want to sell your old horses as colts? Do you want me to teach a mule how to speak French?' "

The Count of Montijo could not contain his laughter.

Then he asked, "And what did Parrón reply to all that? What did he do?"

"The same as Your Excellency—he burst out laughing."

"And you?"

"I, sir, was laughing too, but tears as big as oranges were rolling down my cheeks."

"Go on."

"All at once he held out his hand to me and said, 'My friend, you are the only clever man who has fallen into my power. All the others have been stupid devils who tried to sadden me: they wept, bemoaned their fate, and did other foolish things that put me in a bad humor. Only you have made me laugh, and if it were not for those tears of yours. . . .'

" 'Why, they are tears of joy!'

" 'I believe you. The Devil knows full well that it is the first time I've laughed in the past six or eight years. It is true that I haven't wept, either. But let us settle this: Hey, boys!'

"No sooner had Parrón said this than I was encircled by a swarm of rifles in the twinkling of an eye. I began to scream: 'Lord help me!'

"Parrón said to them: 'Stop! It is not a question of that—yet. I called you to find out what you have taken from this man.'

" 'A burro without a harness.'

" 'Any money?'

" 'Three *duros* and seven *reales*.'

" 'Leave us!'

"They all withdrew. 'Now tell me my fortune,' exclaimed the robber, holding out his hand.

"I took hold of it, and thought a moment. I realized I was in a situation where I had to speak seriously, and

I told him with heartfelt conviction: 'Parrón, sooner or later—whether you take my life or spare it—you will die on the gallows!'

" 'I've known that all along,' answered the bandit with complete calm. 'Tell me when!'

"I began to calculate. 'This man,' I said to myself, 'is going to spare my life; tomorrow I reach Granada and give the alarm; the day after tomorrow they catch him . . . then the trial begins. . . .'

" 'You ask me when?' I said aloud. 'Well, here it is: you will die during the coming month.'

"Parrón shuddered, and so did I as I realized that my vanity as a fortuneteller could result in having my brains blown out!

" 'Well, look you here, gypsy,' Parrón replied, measuring his words. 'You will remain in my power. If during the entire coming month they do not hang me, I shall hang you as surely as they hanged my father! If I die during that time, you shall go free.'

" 'Thanks!' I said to myself. 'He pardons me . . . after death!' And I regretted having made the time so short.

"We agreed on these terms. I was led to a cave, where they shut me in. Parrón mounted his horse and set off through that rough terrain. . . ."

"Ah, now I understand!" exclaimed the Count of Montijo. "Parrón is dead, you have been set free, and therefore you can give us his description. . . ."

"Quite the contrary, General! Parrón is alive, and now comes the blackest part of this story."

2

"A week went by, and the bandit captain did not come back to see me. As far as I could discover, he had not shown himself around there since the afternoon when I told his fortune; this was not unusual, according to one of my guards.

" 'You know,' he told me, 'every so often the chief takes off and doesn't come back until he feels like it. As a matter of fact, we don't know a thing about what he does during his long absences.'

"Meanwhile, as a result of my entreaties and as a reward for telling all the robbers their fortunes— predicting that they would not be hanged, and that they would have a peaceful old age—I had succeeded in getting them to take me out of the cave and tie me to a tree each afternoon, for I was smothering with the heat inside my prison. Needless to say, a couple of guards were always at my side.

"One evening at about six o'clock the robbers who had gone out on duty that day by order of Parrón's second in command returned to the encampment. They brought with them a poor harvest hand about forty or fifty years old, with his hands tied the way the paintings show Our Savior. His wailing would have broken your heart: 'Give me my twenty *duros,*' he was saying. 'If you only knew how hard I have worked for them! The whole summer, reaping under the burning sun! The whole summer, far from my home, my wife and my children. By sweating and suffering a thousand hardships I have saved up that sum to carry us through the coming winter. And now, just when I am on my way back, anxious to embrace them all and pay the debts those poor creatures have incurred in order to eat, how can I lose that money, which to me is a fortune? Mercy, gentlemen! Give me my twenty *duros!* Give them to me, for the sake of the sorrows of Most Holy Mary!'

"A burst of derisive laughter greeted the groans of the poor father. Tied to the tree, I trembled with horror; we gypsies, too, have families.

" 'Don't be crazy,' said one bandit finally, addressing himself to the reaper. 'You do wrong to think about your money when you have bigger problems to worry about. . . .'

" 'What?' said the reaper, unable to comprehend that there could be a greater misfortune than to leave his children without food.

" 'You are in the power of Parrón!'

" 'Parrón? I do not know him . . . I have never heard of him . . . I come from far away. I am from Alicante, and I was working in Seville.'

" 'Well, my friend, Parrón means death. Everyone who falls into our hands must die. So then, make your will in two minutes and commend your soul to God in two more . . . Ready! Aim! . . . You have four minutes.'

" 'I shall use them well. Hear me, for pity's sake.'

" 'Speak.'

" 'I have six children and an unfortunate wife . . . widow, I mean, for I see that I am going to die. I can read in your eyes that you are worse than wild beasts; yes, worse, because animals of the same species do not devour each other . . . Ah, your pardon, gentlemen; I do not know what I am saying . . . Some one of you must be a father! Isn't there a father among you? Do you know what it means to have six children going hungry all winter? Do you know what it means for a mother to watch her children—her own flesh and blood —slowly die, crying: 'I am hungry . . . I am cold?' Gentlemen, the only reason I want to live is for them. What is life for me? A treadmill of toil and trouble. But

I must live for the sake of my children! My children . . . my dear children!'

"And the father, dragging himself along on the ground, raised his face to the robbers. Such a face! It was like that of the holy martyrs thrown to the lions by Nero, the way the preachers tell us. . . .

"The bandits felt something stir within their hearts. They looked at one another, and when they saw that they were all thinking the same thing, one of them dared to put it into words."

"What did he say?" asked the Captain General, deeply stirred by the story.

"He said: 'Men, Parrón must never learn of what we are about to do.'

" 'Never, never,' the bandits stammered.

" 'Be on your way, my good man,' exclaimed one of the bandits, who actually had tears in his eyes.

"And I made signs to the reaper that he should leave at once.

" 'Quick! On your way!' they all repeated, turning their backs to him.

"The reaper put out his hand automatically. 'Aren't you satisfied?' one of them shouted. 'You want your money, too? Go on, go on! Don't try our patience!'

"And the poor father went off weeping. He was soon lost to sight.

"A half hour went by, during which the thieves swore to each other that they would never tell their captain that they had spared a man's life. Suddenly Parrón appeared, with the reaper riding on the rump of his horse. The bandits backed away in astonishment. Parrón dismounted very slowly, unslung his double-barrelled shotgun, and said as he aimed it at his comrades: 'You imbeciles! You scoundrels! I wonder why I don't kill the lot of you! Quick! Give this man the money you stole from him!'

"The thieves took out the twenty *duros* and gave them to the reaper, who threw himself at the feet of that bandit chief who had such a kind heart. . . .

"Parrón said to him: 'God's peace be with you. Without your information I never would have caught them. Now you see that you were wrong to mistrust me. I have fulfilled my promise . . . Here are your twenty *duros* . . . And now, get going!'

"The reaper, overjoyed, embraced him again and again, and then set off. But he had gone hardly fifty paces when his benefactor called him back. The poor man hastened to retrace his steps. 'What is your wish?' he asked, anxious to be of service to the man who had restored happiness to his family.

" 'Do you know Parrón?' the chief asked.

" 'I do not.'

" 'You are wrong!' the bandit replied. 'I am Parrón!'

"The reaper stood there, stunned. Parrón raised his shotgun and fired both barrels at the man, who fell dead to the ground. 'Curse you!' were the only words he uttered.

"Even amid my blinding terror I noted that the tree to which I was tied trembled slightly, and that my bonds were loosening. One of the pellets, after striking the reaper, had cut the rope that tied me to the trunk. I concealed the fact that I was free, and waited for a chance to escape.

"Meanwhile, Parrón was saying to his men: 'Now you can rob him. You are a bunch of fools, a pack of stupid idiots! To let a man go—as he did—shouting along the highway! It's a lucky thing I was the one to meet him and find out what was going on. It might have been the militia, and he would have given your description and revealed our hideout to them—as he did to me—and we would all be in jail now. You see what comes of robbing without killing? Well, that's enough of a lecture for now. Bury that corpse so it won't begin to stink!'

"While the thieves were digging the grave and Parrón was sitting down to have something to eat with his back turned toward me, I slowly crept away from the tree and slid down into a nearby ravine.

"It was nighttime now. Under cover of darkness I made off at top speed, and by the light of the stars I spied my little burro, which was eating there calmly, tied to an oak tree. I mounted, and did not stop until I reached here. Therefore, sir, give me the thousand *reales* and I shall give you the description of Parrón, who kept my three and a half *duros*. . . ."

The gypsy dictated the description of the bandit, and immediately collected the promised reward. He went out of the Captain General's headquarters, leaving the Count of Montijo, and the person present who told me all these details, utterly astonished.

It now remains for us to learn whether Heredia guessed correctly when he told Parrón's fortune.

3

Two weeks after the scene we have just described, at about nine o'clock one morning a large crowd of idlers was standing in the street of San Juan de Dios and part of the street of San Felipe in that same city of Granada, watching the mustering of two companies of militia. They were to leave at half past nine in search of Parrón, whose whereabouts and description, along with those of all his companions in crime, had at last been learned by the Count of Montijo.

Public interest and emotion were unusually keen, and no less extraordinary was the gravity with which the militiamen were taking leave of their friends and families as they marched off on such a serious mission, so great was the fear that Parrón had come to instill in the whole of the former Kingdom of Granada!

"It seems that we are ready to fall in," said one militiaman to another, "and I don't see Corporal López."

"That's really strange, because he always gets here before anyone else when it's a matter of going out to find Parrón, whom he hates with all his heart."

"Well, don't you know what has happened?" said a third militiaman, taking part in the conversation.

"Hello, it's our new comrade . . . How are you getting along in our outfit?"

"Fine!" answered the one addressed. He was a man of pale complexion and distinguished bearing, whose uniform hung loosely upon him.

"So . . . you were saying?" replied the first soldier.

"Ah, yes! I was saying that Corporal López is dead," the pale militiaman answered.

"Manuel, what are you saying? That can't be true!"

"I myself saw López this morning, as surely as I see you now. . . ."

The soldier named Manuel answered coolly, "Parrón killed him a half hour ago."

"Parrón? Where?"

"Right here in Granada! They found López' body at Cuesta del Perro."

All fell silent, and Manuel began to whistle a patriotic air.

"That's eleven militiamen gone in six days!" a sergeant exclaimed. "Parrón has set out to exterminate us! But how is it that he is here in Granada? Weren't we going to look for him in the Sierra de Loja?"

Manuel stopped whistling, and said with his usual indifference, "An old woman who witnessed the crime says that as soon as he killed López he boasted that if we went in search of him we would have the pleasure of meeting him. . . ."

"Comrade, you are astonishingly calm! You speak of Parrón with such scorn. . . ."

"What is Parrón but an ordinary man?" replied Manuel arrogantly.

Just then several voices cried, "Fall in!" The two companies lined up, and the roll call began.

At that moment the gypsy Heredia happened to pass by, and stopped—like everyone else—to look at that splendid troop. Manuel, the new militiaman, was seen to give a start and step back a bit, as if to conceal himself behind his companions. At the same time Heredia riveted his gaze upon him and gave a shout; then, jumping as if a snake had bitten him, he began to run toward San Jerónimo Street.

Manuel raised his rifle and aimed at the gypsy . . . But a militiaman had time to deflect the weapon and the shot went wild in the air.

"He is crazy! Manuel has gone mad! A soldier has lost his mind!" the crowd of witnesses to that scene shouted in a swelling chorus.

Officers, sergeants and civilians surrounded the soldier, who struggled to escape and who for this reason was held even more firmly. He was showered with questions, denunciations and insults, which drew from him not a word in reply. Meanwhile, Heredia had been seized in the plaza of the University by some passersby, who took him for a malefactor when they saw him running away after the shot rang out.

"Take me to the Captain General's headquarters!" the gypsy said. "I must speak to the Count of Montijo!"

"What do you mean, the Count of Montijo! A likely story!" his captors answered. "Here come the soldiers, and they will see what is to be done with you!"

"That's all right with me," answered Heredia, "but be careful Parrón doesn't kill me."

"Parrón? What does this fellow mean?"

"Come, and you shall see."

So saying, the gypsy had them take him to the commander of the militia unit. Pointing to Manuel, he said: "Sir, that man is Parrón, and I am the gypsy who gave his description to the Count of Montijo two weeks ago."

"Parrón! Parrón has been captured! One of the soldiers was Parrón!" shouted many voices.

"I don't doubt it," said the commander meanwhile, as he read the description given to him by the Captain General. "We have certainly been stupid! But who would have thought to look for the bandit chief among the very soldiers who were going out to capture him?"

"Fool that I am!" exclaimed Parrón as he looked at the gypsy with eyes like a wounded lion's. "He is the only man whose life I spared. I deserve my fate!"

The next week they hanged Parrón. The gypsy's fortune, then, came true completely.

All of which—let it be said in fitting conclusion—does not mean that you should believe in the infallibility of such prophecies. Even less does it mean that Parrón's procedure of killing everyone who came to know him was correct. It means only that the ways of Providence are inscrutable to man's mind—and in my opinion no doctrine could be more orthodox than that.

Gustavo Adolfo Bécquer (1836–1870)

. . . was born in Seville, "Queen of Andalusia," a city rich in Moorish tradition. His father, an artist, came from a distinguished—but impoverished—family that had emigrated to Spain from Flanders in the sixteenth century. Left an orphan at the age of nine, young Gustavo was brought up by his uncle, who was also an artist. The lad learned to draw and to paint almost before he learned to write. His godmother would have financed him in a business career, but the sensitive young man, who had already begun to compose poetry, left Seville for Madrid at seventeen. He eked out a miserable existence in the capital at painting, translating from French, writing short stories, and illustrating his articles for the daily newspapers. He starved, of course, and his privations led him to that scourge of many nineteenth-century Romantic poets and artists, tuberculosis. An unhappy marriage—followed by separation and a hopeless love-affair—further complicated his already tragic life. A deep melancholy possessed his soul. He died in Madrid at the age of thirty-four.

During these years he had been composing occasional poetry. His seventy-six semi-autobiographical *Rhymes* were published posthumously by friends. They became the most famous sequence of love poems in the Spanish language, and influenced all subsequent poets, including the great masters of the Generation of 1898 and of contemporary Spain, as well as the Modernists in Spanish America. Diaphanous, bittersweet, disarmingly simple in their choice of words, they are pure poetry at its very best.

Bécquer poured into his prose all the luxuriance of language that he held in check in his poetry. He often illustrated his prose works with excellent sketches that reveal the great sensitivity of the handsome, nostalgic young artist-poet. His most famous prose collections are his letters of literary criticism and his group of twenty-two *Legends*. These are rich in Andalusian local color, customs, and traditions; most have elements of the macabre, the magical, and the mysterious. He was, in fact, a belated Romantic; almost all his stories breathe the spirit of the Middle Ages, and abound in crumbling castles, Gothic cathedrals, and supernatural manifestations. The following selection, translated from these *Legends*, is typical of Bécquer's beautiful, poetic prose.

The Kiss

WHEN ONE PORTION of the French army occupied historic Toledo at the beginning of this century, their general staff, well aware of the dangers to the troops if they were scattered and billeted in separate houses in Spanish towns, issued orders that the biggest and best buildings in the city should be taken over as living quarters. After having occupied the magnificent Alcázar of Charles V, they seized the City Hall; and when the latter could hold no more men they began to take over the cloisters of the religious orders. Finally they went so far as to transform into stables even churches consecrated to holy worship.

This was the state of affairs in the city in which the incident I am about to relate took place, when one night—it was quite late—about a hundred of their dragoons rode into town. They were tall, bold, and well-built—our grandmothers still tell us about them with admiration—and were muffled up in their dark military cloaks. With the clanking of their weapons and the noisy clatter of the horses' hoofs, which struck sparks against the cobblestones, they made a deafening din as they wound through the narrow, deserted streets from the Puerta del Sol to Zocodover Plaza.

The group was under the command of an officer who was quite young. He was riding some thirty paces ahead of his men, and was speaking in a low tone to a man who was also a soldier, as evidenced by his uniform. The latter, who was walking in front of the officer and carrying a lantern in his hand, was apparently serving as a guide through the confusing labyrinth of dark, winding streets.

"In truth," the rider was saying to his escort, "if the quarters being set aside for us are as you describe them, it would almost be preferable to camp out in the fields, or in the middle of the plaza."

"What can you expect, captain?" answered the guide, who was in fact a billeting sergeant. "Not even one more grain of wheat can fit into the Alcázar, let alone a man. And let's not even mention the convent of San Juan de los Reyes, where there are some friars' cells that are billeting fifteen men! The convent to which I am taking you wasn't a bad spot until about three or four days ago; then one of our flying columns that are patrolling the province dropped in on us out of the blue. Thank Heaven we were able to crowd them into the cloisters and leave the church itself vacant."

"Oh, well!" the officer exclaimed after a short silence, as if resigning himself to the strange billet that chance was forcing upon them. "Better these uncomfortable quarters than none at all. Anyway, if it rains—and the way the clouds are piling up it easily may—we'll be under cover, and that's something."

The conversation was broken off at this point, and the horsemen, preceded by the guide, followed along in silence until they came to a small plaza. Beyond it loomed the black silhouette of the convent, with its Moorish tower, its belfry, its vaulted cupola and its tile roofs with their dark, uneven outlines.

"Here are your lodgings, sir," called the quartermaster when he saw him.

After halting his troop, the captain dismounted. Taking the lantern from the guide, he went toward the spot the latter was pointing out. Inasmuch as the convent's church had been completely dismantled, the soldiers who were occupying the rest of the building considered the doors quite useless, and they had been tearing them apart board by board each day to build bonfires so as to keep warm at night. Our young officer, then, had no need to use keys or to open bolts in order to gain entrance to the interior of the church.

The lantern's flickering rays, fading back into the deep gloom of the nave and aisles, enlarged the quartermaster's shadow to gigantic proportions and projected it grotesquely against the wall. With the sergeant preceding him, the officer roamed up and down the church, peering into its deserted chapels one by one. As soon as he had examined the entire premises, he ordered his men to dismount and lodged them—horses and men intermingled—as best he could.

As we have said, the church was completely dismantled. The torn strips of veiling with which the monks had covered the main altar when they left that holy place were still hanging from its high cornices. Scattered along the aisles and leaning against the walls were some altar pieces without statues in their niches; in the dark choir loft a ribbon of light revealed the eerie outlines of the carved wooden stalls; and in the stone floor, which was broken in several spots, one could see broad flagstone burial markers covered with crests, coats-of-arms and lengthy Gothic inscriptions. Back in the depths of the silent chapels, and far off in the area where the transept crossed the nave, the vague outlines of stone statues stood out still and white like ghosts in the gloom. Lying there atop their marble tombs, or on their knees in prayer, they seemed to be the sole inhabitants of the ruined building. Anyone with the slightest spark of imagination, and who was less exhausted than the officer of dragoons—he had ridden fourteen long leagues that day—or anyone less accustomed to looking upon such sacrilege as an everyday occurrence, would have been unable to close his eyes all night in that dark and awesome structure. The cursing of the soldiers, who were complaining loudly about their improvised barracks, the metallic clink of their spurs resounding upon the flagstones over the crypts in the floor, the noise of the horses pawing impatiently, shaking their heads and rattling the chains that fastened them to the stone pillars, all produced strange and fearsome sounds that spread through the confines of the church and rose to mingle in confused echoes that reverberated among its lofty vaults.

But our hero, though young, was accustomed to these vicissitudes of campaign life. As soon as he had bedded down his men he ordered a makeshift bed of hay placed at the foot of the stair leading to the chancel, wrapped himself up in his cloak as best he could, placed his head on the first step, and within five minutes was snoring as peacefully as Joseph Bonaparte himself in the royal palace at Madrid.[1]

The soldiers, using their saddles as pillows, imitated his example, and little by little the murmur of their voices died down. Within a half hour there could be heard only the muffled moaning of the wind as it blew through the broken panes of the Gothic windows, the frightened fluttering of the night birds that had their nests on the stone ledge over the sculptured figures

---

[1] Napoleon had placed his brother Joseph on the throne of Spain after the French troops invaded the peninsula.

along the walls, and the sound of the sentinel's steps as he paced the portico back and forth, muffled in the ample folds of his military cloak.

2

Back in the days of this strange but truthful tale, the city of Toledo, for those unable to appreciate the artistic treasures within its ancient walls—and this is as true today as it was then—was just a shabby, dull moldering old town.

To judge by the acts of vandalism that left sad and imperishable evidence of their occupation, the French army officers were anything but artists or antiquarians, and it goes without saying that they were supremely bored in the ancient city of the Caesars.[2]

With their morale in this condition, the most insignificant piece of news that came to break the quiet sameness of those interminable, monotonous days was seized upon avidly by the idle soldiers. Thus the promotion of one of their comrades to the next higher grade, the news of the strategic deployment of one of their flying columns, the departure of a royal messenger, or the arrival of any military unit in the city, was converted into a fertile topic of conversation and became the object of all kinds of comment until another incident came along to take its place and serve as the basis for new complaints, gossip and rumors.

As was to be expected, the arrival of the dragoons

[2] Toledo, on the Tagus River, was conquered by the Romans about 193 B.C. It was the capital of Visigothic Spain, and was then under Moorish domination until 1085. Toledo was the capital of all Spain until superseded by Madrid in the sixteenth century. The richness of its artistic and architectural treasures can be inferred from these successive occupations. El Greco made his home in Toledo, and his most famous masterpiece—*El entierro del Conde de Orgaz*—hangs in a church there.

(whose commander we left in the preceding chapter sleeping soundly and recovering from the hardships of his journey) was the sole topic of conversation among the officers who went the following day as usual to enjoy the sunshine and chat awhile in Zocodover Plaza. The conversation had been revolving about this subject for about an hour. One of those present, a former schoolmate of the newly arrived officer, had made an appointment to meet him in the plaza, and the latter's absence was already being interpreted in several ways when our dashing young captain appeared from one of the side streets. He had taken off his bulky military cloak, and was wearing a dark blue tunic trimmed with red, a huge helmet with a crest of white feathers, and a magnificent cavalry saber encased in a steel scabbard that clanked as it bounced along in rhythm with his martial gait and the sharp, metallic clink of his golden spurs.

As soon as his friend saw the captain he went up to greet him, accompanied by almost all those who made up the group. The accounts they had heard about his strange, unusual character had aroused their curiosity and made them want to meet him.

After the usual hearty embraces and the joyful shouts, congratulations and questions that are customary at such meetings, and after talking at great length about the latest news reports in Madrid, the changing fortunes of war, and good friends who had been killed or transferred, the conversation—which had been skipping from one subject to another—finally got around to the inevitable topic: personal gripes about the army, the lack of amusements in the city, and objections to the billeting arrangements.

At this point one of the group, who apparently had

heard of the bad grace with which the young officer resigned himself to billeting his men in the abandoned church, said to him banteringly, "Speaking of quarters, how did you make out last night in those assigned to you?"

"Not too badly," answered the captain. "Although it's true I didn't sleep very much, the source of my insomnia was worth the trouble. To stay awake because one is near a beautiful woman is surely not the worst thing that could happen."

"A woman!" his questioners repeated, surprised at the new arrival's good fortune. "That's certainly lucky for you, so soon after getting here!"

"Maybe it's an old sweetheart from Madrid who came down to Toledo just to make his banishment more bearable," added another member of the group.

"Oh, no!" the captain said. "Not at all. I swear, on my honor as an officer and a gentleman, that I did not know her, and that I never thought I'd find such a lovely lady in such miserable surroundings. It's a regular adventure story."

"Tell us about it! Tell us!" exclaimed the officers in one voice as they crowded around the captain. And since the latter seemed ready to do so, they all paid the closest attention to his words as he began the story in the following way:

"I was sleeping last night as only a man can sleep after a long, hard day of riding. In the dead of night I was suddenly awakened with a start by a horrible noise— such a noise that as I propped up on one elbow I was deafened for a moment. It left my ears ringing for about a minute, as if a huge horse-fly were buzzing close to them.

"As you may have imagined, the cause of my fright

was my first experience in hearing that infernal *Campana Gorda,* a kind of bronze bell the clergy of Toledo have hung in their cathedral with the praiseworthy purpose of annoying the life out of all who need some sleep. Swearing under my breath at the bell and the bellringer, I was getting ready—once that fantastic and frightful din had stopped—to renew my interrupted sleep, when an extraordinary sight stunned my senses as it appeared before my eyes. By the fitful moonlight filtering into the church through the narrow, mullioned window in the main chapel, I saw a woman kneeling near the altar."

The officers looked at one another with expressions that varied from astonishment to disbelief. The captain, paying no attention to the effect his narrative was producing, continued in these words:

"You simply cannot imagine anything to compare with that eerie, nocturnal vision shimmering in the shadowy gloom of the chapel, like the Virgins depicted on stained glass windows you have doubtless seen standing out all white and glowing from afar against the dark background of a cathedral. Her oval face, which showed signs of a slight spiritual gauntness; her regular features, with their gentle, melancholy sweetness; her deep pallor, the clean lines of her slender figure, her calm, noble expression and her white, flowing gown all conjured up memories of the ladies of my boyhood dreams—chaste, celestial visions, fancied objects of my vague, adolescent affections!

"I thought myself the victim of an hallucination, and with my eyes fixed steadily upon her I dared not even breathe, for fear that one faint breath might break the spell. She remained motionless. It occurred to me as I gazed upon her there, so diaphanous and radiant, that she was not of this world, but was instead a spirit that had taken human form for a moment and had come down on that beam of moonlight. In the air all about her there was a bluish glow that sloped down from the high, mullioned window to the base of the wall opposite, piercing the sepulchral gloom of that mournful, mysterious place."

One of his former schoolmates, who had at first considered the story just a joke but had become more interested in the narrative as it went along, exclaimed: "But how did the woman come to be there? Didn't you say anything to her? Didn't she explain her presence in that place?"

"I decided not to speak to her, because I had concluded that she was not going to answer me—or see me, or hear me."

"Was she deaf?"

"Was she dumb?"

"Was she blind?" several of those who were listening to the story blurted out together.

There was a short pause, and then the captain declared: "She was all those things, because she was . . . a marble statue!"

When the group heard the amazing conclusion to that strange adventure they all burst into raucous laughter. One of them—the only one who had listened quietly and seriously to the tale as it was told—said to the captain:

"All very well and good! But if that's the kind of woman she is, I have dozens of them—a regular harem —in the church of San Juan de los Reyes. From this point on, I place the whole harem at your disposal, since apparently it makes no difference to you whether a woman is flesh and blood—or made of stone!"

"Oh, no!" replied the captain, who was not in the least disturbed by the laughter of his comrades. "I'm sure they are not like mine. She is a real Castilian lady who, through some miracle of the sculptor's art, appears not to be buried inside that tomb, but to be alive and breathing, kneeling there motionless upon her sepulchre, with her hands clasped in prayer and lost in mystic rapture."

"The way you explain it, you'll end up by convincing us that the fable of Galatea is true!"

"For my part, I can assure you that I have always thought the fable ridiculous; but since last night I have begun to understand Pygmalion's passion."

"In view of the special nature of your new lady love, I'm sure you will not object to introducing us to her. Speaking for myself, I can hardly wait to meet this marvelous creature. . . . But what in blazes is eating you? It almost looks as though you're afraid to introduce us. Ha, ha! Things have reached a pretty pass if you're even jealous. . . ."

"Jealous?" the captain replied quickly. "So far as mortal men are concerned, no . . . but still in all . . . just let me tell you how far my madness has gone. Next to the figure of this woman there is another marble statue that also seems to be alive: it is a stern warrior . . . her husband, no doubt. Well—and now I'm going to tell you everything, even though you may laugh and think me foolish—if I hadn't been afraid of being called a madman, I'd have smashed him into a hundred little pieces."

A new and even more uproarious burst of laughter from the officers greeted this bizarre revelation by the eccentric admirer of the stone lady.

"That does it! We simply must see her!" said some.

"Yes, indeed! We have to see whether the adored object merits such deep love!" added others.

"When are we getting together for a drink in the church where you are quartered?" exclaimed the rest.

"Whenever you like—tonight, if you wish," answered the young captain; and his customary smile, dispelled for a moment by that outburst of jealousy, returned to his face. "By the way: in my baggage I brought a couple of dozen bottles of champagne—real champagne; they are what is left of a present given to our general, who, as you know, is distantly related to me."

"Bravo! Bravo!" the officers exclaimed with one voice as they broke into joyous whoops.

"We'll have some wine from the old country!"

"And we'll sing one of Ronsard's songs!"

"And we'll talk about women . . . apropos of our host's lady love."

"So then . . . until tonight!"

"Till tonight!"

3

The peaceful inhabitants of Toledo had long since closed and bolted the heavy doors of their fine old homes. The big bell of the cathedral was tolling the hour of curfew, and atop the Alcázar, which had been converted into a barracks, the bugler was just sounding the final notes of taps when ten or twelve officers, who had been arriving in ones and twos at the Zocodover Plaza, started out together along the road that leads from there to the convent where the captain was quartered. They were spurred on more by their anticipation of draining the bottles they had been promised than by their wish to see the marvelous statue.

Night had closed in dark and threatening, with lead-bellied clouds scudding across the sky. The captive wind, sobbing through the narrow, winding streets, caused flickering altar lights to dim, and made screaking weathervanes shrill sharply as they turned atop their towers.

As soon as the officers came into view across the square in which their new friend's quarters were located, the captain came out to greet them. He had been awaiting them impatiently, and after exchanging a few words in a low tone they all went inside the church. In its cloistral darkness the lantern's dim light strove to pierce the deep, black shadows.

"Upon my word!" one of the guests exclaimed as he looked about him. "This is hardly the most suitable place in the world for a party!"

"Quite right," said another. "You are inviting us to meet a lady, and it's all we can do to see our hands before our eyes!"

"And above all," added a third, pulling his cloak about him, "it's so cold in here it seems as though we're in Siberia."

"Easy does it, gentlemen, easy does it!" their host interrupted. "Everything will be provided." And turning to one of his orderlies, he continued: "Private, look for a little wood around here, and build us a big bonfire in the main chapel!"

The orderly, obeying his captain's orders, began to hack away at the choir stalls and soon had gathered a large quantity of firewood that he kept piling at the foot of the steps leading to the chancel. Using the lantern, he proceeded to kindle an auto-da-fe with those richly-carved fragments, and through the flames one could catch an occasional glimpse of a fluted column, the figure of some saintly abbot, a woman's torso, or the misshapen head of a griffin peering out from leafy scrollwork. Within a few minutes a bright glow that suddenly lighted up the whole church announced to the officers that it was time to begin the festivities.

The captain, doing the honors in his quarters with as much ceremony as in his own home, turned to his guests and said, "Gentlemen, shall we repair to the refreshment table?"

His comrades, affecting great solemnity, answered his invitation with a mock-heroic bow and proceeded to the main chapel. The founder of the feast, who was walking ahead of them, stopped a moment when he reached the steps. Extending his arm toward the spot occupied by the sepulchre, he said to them with punctilious formality, "It gives me great pleasure to present you to the lady of my dreams. I think you will agree that I have not exaggerated her beauty."

The officers turned their eyes toward the spot indicated by their friend, and an involuntary gasp of amazement escaped their lips. There in a burial vault lined with black marble, they beheld the statue of a woman more beautiful indeed than any ever created by a sculptor's hand. On her knees in prayer, and with her face turned toward the altar, she was more regally beautiful than man's mortal wish could conjure up.

"In truth, she is an angel," exclaimed one of the officers.

"Too bad she's made of marble!" added another. "There's no doubt that even the illusion of being near a woman like that is enough to keep you awake all night."

"And you don't know who she is?" some of the officers examining the statue asked the captain, who was smiling in satisfaction at his triumph.

"Recalling a little of the Latin I learned as a boy," he answered, "I have—with difficulty—succeeded in deciphering the inscription on the tomb. From what I can make out, she is the wife of a Castilian nobleman, a famous warrior who campaigned with the Great Captain.³ I have forgotten the warrior's name, but his wife, whom you see there, was Doña Elvira de Castañeda, and if the copy is anything like the original, I'll swear she must have been the most remarkable woman of her century!"

After this brief explanation the guests, who had not lost sight of their main reason for the gathering, proceeded to uncork some of the bottles, and the wine began to circulate freely as they sat about the fire.

As the rounds of drinks became more frequent and the bubbling champagne began to turn their heads, the young men's animation and their boisterous shouting kept increasing. Some of them tossed the empty bottles at the granite monks carved into the pillars of the church, others sang ribald drinking songs at the top of their lungs, while still others burst into gales of laughter, clapped their hands in applause, or argued among themselves with blasphemous oaths.

The captain drank in dejected silence, without taking his eyes off the statue of Doña Elvira. Her marble likeness, illumined by the bonfire's reddish glow and seen through the muddled blear of his intoxicated gaze, appeared to be transformed at times into a living woman. It seemed to him that her lips were moving in murmured prayer, that her bosom was heaving with suppressed sobs, that she clasped her hands more tightly,

³ Gonzalo Fernández de Córdoba, "el Gran Capitán," (1453–1515) was a famous Spanish general who fought in many campaigns against the Moors. At Cerignola, Italy, in 1503 his troops defeated the French, and gained for Spain the Kingdom of Naples.

and that her cheeks grew pink as if she were blushing at that shocking, sacrilegious scene.

The officers, who had noticed their comrade's maudlin silence, stirred him from the trance into which he had fallen. Handing him a goblet, they called in chorus: "Come on! Offer a toast! You are the only one who hasn't done so all evening!"

The young man struggled to his feet and took the goblet. Raising it on high, and turning to face the statue of the warrior who knelt at the side of Doña Elvira, he exclaimed:

"I drink to the Emperor Napoleon, and to the success of his arms, thanks to which we have been able to come down into Castile and court in her very tomb the wife of the victor in the Battle of Cerignola!"

The soldiers greeted the toast with a burst of applause, and the captain took a few staggering steps toward the sepulchre. Then, with the befuddled smile so typical of intoxication, he continued addressing the warrior's statue:

"Don't think I bear you any ill-will because I consider you a rival . . . on the contrary, I admire you as a patient, long-suffering husband, a model of forbearance, and I in my turn wish to be generous. You, as a soldier, must have been a drinking man, too . . . let it not be said that I let you die of thirst watching us drink up twenty bottles. Here, take this!"

So saying, and after raising the goblet of champagne to his own lips in order to moisten them, he dashed the rest into the statue's face. Then he burst into uproarious laughter as he watched the wine drip down upon the tomb from the stone beard of the motionless warrior.

"Captain!" exclaimed one of his comrades, jokingly. "Watch what you're doing! These jests with stone statues can be costly, you know. Remember what happened to the 5th Hussars in the monastery of Poblet, where—so they say—the dead warriors drew their granite swords one night and set about the men who were amusing themselves by drawing black mustaches on them."

The young officers greeted this story with wild hoots of laughter. But the captain paid no attention to them, and with his mind fixed steadily on his objective, continued speaking:

"Do you think I'd have given him the wine if I didn't know he'd swallow at least the little that entered his mouth? Oh, no! I don't believe—as you do—that statues are just pieces of marble, as lifeless today as when they were taken from the quarry. Artists, who are almost gods, infuse into their works a breath of life which does not enable them to walk and move, but which undoubtedly gives them a strange kind of life we cannot understand, a kind of life I cannot explain but which I can feel, especially when I have been drinking a little."

"Fine!" his comrades exclaimed. "Have another drink, and keep on!"

The captain drank again, and with his eyes fixed on Doña Elvira he continued with growing animation:

"Look at her! Look at her! Don't you see those iridescent tones of pink on her clear, delicate flesh? Doesn't it look as though there is a rose-colored, liquid light flowing beneath that thin, blue skin, smooth as alabaster? Could you ask for more life than that? Could you ask for greater reality?"

"Yes, indeed!" said one of his listeners. "We could wish that she were flesh and blood."

"Flesh and blood? Women like that are cheap and

rotten! In drunken revels I have felt my lips and head aflame; I have felt fire flow foaming through my veins like molten lava whose fetid fumes befuddle and bemuse men's minds and make them see strange visions. Then a kiss from those women of flesh and blood would sear me like a burning brand, and I would thrust them away from me with disgust and horror, and even loathing. Because then—as now—I needed a breath of sea breeze for my burning brow, I needed to drink ice and kiss snow . . . snow tinted with a soft light . . . snow bathed in golden sunbeams . . . a woman who is cool, and white, and lovely, like that woman made of marble who seems to incite me with her fantastic beauty, who seems to sway in rhythm with the flames and tempt me with her moving lips that offer me her treasured love . . . Oh, yes! . . . one kiss . . . one single kiss from her could cool the ardor that consumes me . . ."

And with a wild, dazed look upon his face he started toward the statue with unsteady steps.

"Captain!" cried some of the officers who were watching. "What madness is this? Stop the joke, and leave the dead in peace!"

The young man did not even hear what they were saying. Staggering on as best he could, he reached the tomb and drew close to the statue; but as he stretched out his arms a shriek of horror echoed through the church. With blood streaming from his mouth and nose and eyes, he had collapsed at the foot of the sepulchre, his face all smashed. The officers, speechless with terror, dared not move a step to help him.

At the moment their comrade tried to bring his burning lips close to those of Doña Elvira, they had seen the motionless warrior raise his fist and strike the captain down with a frightful blow of his stone gauntlet.

NOTES

NOTES

NOTES